All the
Wrong Moves

Also by Nikki Carter

Step to This
It Is What It Is
It's All Good
Cool Like That
Not a Good Look

Published by Dafina Books

Acknowledgments

First and foremost, I thank God for making this entire journey possible; for giving me the opportunity to live out my dreams! He is so awesome!

My family is the bomb.com! To my husband, Brent: You already know what it is. Thank you for all you do. Briana and Brittany, thanks for being great readers and book critics. I love y'all. Brynn, Fatman, and Brooke, thank you for being good so Mommy can write!

Thank you to the BEST editor in the business: Mercedes Fernandez. You manage to be cool and professional at the same time. Do you, boo! (I'm done, so you can retract your claws and bunny fangs.) Thank you also to Selena, Adeola, and the whole team at Kensington who make these books possible.

A huge thanks to my literary agent, Pattie Steele-Perkins! You rock. Thank you for your words of wisdom and support. Thanks also to Maria Ruvalcaba Hackett for seeing the potential in my work! Hope to do great things with both of you!

Thanks to my sister-friends, Tiffany T, Kymmie, Afrika, Brandi, Leslie, Shawana, and Lil' Robin. Y'all are the best!! Love y'all.

I am so blessed to have a circle of authors around me who have my back, who talk me down from any given scenario, and who help promote my work. Hollerations and blessings to my homegirls Rhonda McKnight, Sherri Lewis, ReShonda Tate Billingsley, Michelle Stimpson, Angela Benson, Tia McCollors, and Miranda Parker.

Thanks to the hilarious bloggers who keep me posted on all the celebrity gossip! Sandrarose.com, Bossip.com, Theybf.com, Crunktastical.net, and Mediatakeout.com. I have to know what's going on in the hood. LOL. Thank you!

To my readers! Love y'all. The notes and the wall posts on Facebook keep me going. Thank you so much for spending your birthday and Christmas money on my books ☺ ! Hope y'all like this one.

Happy reading!

1

"Come on, Sunday. Give it your all. I know you can push this song out."

I take a deep breath and close my eyes. Maybe it's the fact that I'm recording my very first single on my very first album that's got me totally twisted.

Maybe it's the fact that mega-super R & B star Mystique is producing the song and is my mentor! Her words of encouragement are not helping, even though she has a smile on her face.

Mystique continues, "Sunday, I know you've got it in you. I've heard you sing the mess out of this song. Do you need me to leave?"

I shake my head no.

"Do you want me to come in the booth with you?"

I cock my head to one side and shrug. I don't know if that will help, but at this point I'm willing to try anything because I'm tired, hungry, and thirsty.

Sam, the recording engineer and my sort-of crush says over the microphone, "I'm taking a break. Y'all let me know when you're ready."

I feel the tension leave my body when Sam walks out of the recording room. Oh no! That's it! Sam is the reason I can't get this song right.

"Talk to me, mama," Mystique says as she steps into the tiny recording booth. "You seem a little stressed today."

I play with my ponytail nervously. "I-I don't know what it is."

Mystique smiles. "I think you know what it is, and you don't want to tell me."

"Okay . . . maybe you're right."

"Does it have anything to do with that video on You-Tube?"

I sigh at the thought of that video. It was the night of rapper Truth's release party at Club Pyramids, here in Atlanta. It was a hot mess of an evening.

Sam was pissed because I wouldn't be his "official girl," so he was tripping and dancing all crazy on some groupie chicks. Truth, who goes out with my cousin Dreya, took that as his opportunity to push up on me yet again, even though I'd told him no a hundred times. But since Sam was acting a fool with the groupies, I acted an even bigger fool and danced with Truth, knowing that Sam would flip the heck out.

And he definitely flipped out.

He bloodied Truth's face up right before his show, and although the concert went on, the fight was the biggest news of the night. Somebody had used the video camera on his phone to capture the whole thing.

It was on YouTube before we even got home that night.

Ever since then, I've been trying to make it up to Sam. We're supposed to be going to prom together, but it's in three weeks and Sam still isn't speaking to me.

"I guess it has a little bit to do with the video," I admit to Mystique.

"Listen. You guys can't let that stuff get to you. If I got upset about everything that's on the Internet about me and my man, I'd never get any sleep."

"Yeah, but the blogs only have rumors about you! They don't have anything concrete. They've got video of me."

Mystique places a hand on my arm. "It's just your first lesson in being in the limelight. Just remember that someone is always watching."

"That's the problem! I don't know if I want that! I just want to be a normal teenager."

"There are pros and cons to being a celebrity. But I wouldn't trade it for anything, Sunday! I've traveled the world, met the president, and I have millions of fans who care about me. Do you know I got three hundred thousand birthday cards?"

I laugh out loud. "Wow! Really?"

"Yes. And you'll have the same thing. You're so talented, and I know you can do this."

"But this song . . . it's about a girl having a crush on a guy. It's just hard to do with Sam out there mean mugging me."

"Yeah, guys have pretty fragile egos. He's just hurt right now, I guess."

"But why the double standard? I didn't trip about his groupie chicks."

Mystique chuckles. "From what I heard you did trip! You danced with Truth? Girl, you know that was messy."

"It was messy, wasn't it?"

"Just talk to Sam. Admit you were wrong, and then maybe y'all can get back to being friends again."

"You think so?"

"Yeah, but I need you to do it quickly, so we can record this single."

Sam walks back into the studio and says over the mic, "You ready, Sunday?"

I glance at Mystique, and she nods. "Sam, I need to make a phone call. Can you hold on a sec?" she asks.

She winks at me on the way out of the booth and mouths, "Talk to him."

I bite my lip as I try to get up the courage to talk to Sam. He seems to be deep in thought as he plays what sounds like random notes on the keyboard. I know him, though, so it's not random. He's got a melody in his head.

I step out of the booth and ask, "Working on something new?"

"What? Oh, naw. Not feeling inspired too much."

"Lost your muse?" I ask.

That was an inside joke, but Sam doesn't laugh. We worked so well together writing the songs on Dreya's album that he'd started calling me his muse.

"Yeah, I guess so," he replies.

I clear my throat, trying to think of a way to start this conversation. "Y'all video got twenty thousand hits on YouTube."

Sam gives me a crazy look. Why in the world did I say that? OMG! Open mouth and insert foot.

"Twenty thousand people saw me puttin' work in on Truth. Sweet."

"You're such a guy."

"Yeah. I am."

"You did kinda put a beat down on him, though."

Sam frowns. "Wish I hadn't done it, though. It wasn't worth it."

"I wasn't worth fighting for?" I ask. "Wow."

"Well, why should I be fighting over a girl who doesn't want to be with me? That doesn't make a lot of sense."

"Sam, I never said I didn't want to be your girl."

"You never said you did."

This conversation is going in circles. "So, are we not friends anymore now? 'Cause I still want us to be friends, Sam."

"I guess we can be friends, but you're gonna have to give me a while to get over the whole thing with Truth. When I see him, I just want to punch him again."

"You can't do that! I need . . . I mean we need you on the tour."

"Y'all don't need me. I'm the studio engineer and producer. I can stay here over the summer."

I touch Sam's shoulder and feel him flinch. "Sam, can you imagine how crazy that's gonna be for me if I have to be on tour with Dreya, Truth, and Bethany, without you? As a matter of fact, I'm gonna pull out if you don't go."

"Are you crazy? You can't pull out of the tour. Mystique and Epsilon Records would trip."

"I'm not going unless you go."

"It's not that serious, Sunday."

"Yes, it is."

He sighs. "All right, cool. I'll go."

"Yay!" I kiss Sam on the cheek, and he flinches again. "Don't . . ."

"Friends don't kiss each other on the cheek?"

"I don't want your lips on me."

I give him a smart-aleck smirk. "That's not true. You soooo want my lips on you."

"Sunday, don't play with my emotions."

"Okay, I'll stop. But can I ask you one more thing?"

"What?"

"Are we still going to prom together?"

Sam puffs his cheeks with air and taps a few notes on the keyboard. I can tell he's trying to think of an answer.

"I mean, it's okay if you don't . . ." I say.

"It's not that I don't want to, but I got so angry with you that I asked another girl at my school to go to my prom."

"Oh." I blink a few times because I refuse to let a tear drop. He asked someone else? He could've told me before he did that. I thought we were better than that. I guess I was wrong.

"You didn't ask someone else?" he asks.

"No. I thought we'd make up by the time prom came."

"Do you still want me to go to your prom with you?"

I shrug. "If you want to, I guess. I don't have a date."

Sam flashes a bright smile. "Okay. We can go as friends."

"Right. As friends."

Mystique comes back into the recording room. "Are we ready to record now?"

"Yes," I reply. "Let's do this."

2

---

*Don't take your love away from me / Don't break
me down / Don't break, don't make me over I can't
see / Don't make, don't make, make me cry*
—Sunday Tolliver

The Epsilon Records summer tour is going to be hot to
death, with headliners Truth and Drama (my cousin
Dreya) and me opening up the show. It's tripped out how
we're going on tour as almost superstars and we still live
in our same house in Decatur, Georgia. Dreya, her mom
Charlie, and my little cousin Manny all stay with me and
my mom.

We've gotten a little advance money, but not enough to
change our lives. Especially since I'm going to Spelman
College in the fall. I'm stacking all my paper so that I
don't have to take out student loans, or beg my mama for
money.

Dreya, on the other hand, has probably blown through
her entire advance. She bought some jewelry and de-
signer clothes, and whenever she or her mother run low
on funds they call up our manager Big D. He makes sure
they get what they need, but I know that somewhere,

somebody is keeping a tally on all this money they're blowing through.

I watch in silence as Dreya, who everybody else calls by her stage name Drama, and my ex-best friend Bethany plan out prom. I'm at the dining room table pretending to do some homework, and they're chilling on the living room couch.

Dreya runs her hand through her short spiky hair. Something she does when she's thinking hard. "We're gonna rent a Lambo," Dreya says.

"That's hot!" Bethany replies. She's so bubbly with her response that her long, high ponytail bounces from side to side.

"And we'll call Big D and see if the BET video crew wants to tape it for our reality show."

"Isn't the reality show supposed to be about the tour?" Bethany asks.

Earlier this year, Truth and Dreya performed on BET's *106 & Park* as part of a new artist showcase. The crowd showed so much love that BET thought it would be a good idea to do a reality show based on the tour. Of course, Epsilon Records thought it was a great idea! We'd be able to promote our albums on BET and get kids pumped about the tour. It was a win-win.

Dreya sees the reality show as a way to blow up, and I agree with her. But I don't want to have anyone video-taping any craziness associated with me! The YouTube fight video between Truth and Sam was bad enough. I'm just trying to figure out a way to follow Mystique's advice and stay low key.

Bethany twirls her index finger around a stray curl in

her hair and asks, "So what are you and Truth wearing? I don't want us to clash! I think Romell and I are wearing red."

"We're wearing platinum and white, of course! Truth is gonna look so hot in that white tux. I can't wait to see those girls drooling over my husband!"

Okay, Bethany talking about what she's wearing to prom with my ex-boyfriend Romell, is beyond annoying. I know she's got major beef with me because she didn't get a record deal. It wasn't my fault that Epsilon Records didn't discover her too. Just because me, Bethany, and Dreya were all in a singing group together doesn't mean that we were all destined to be stars.

I don't even know if I want to be a star.

But what I do know is that Bethany is such the opposite of a best friend. She pushed up on Sam, and she's kicking it with Romell. It's like she lives in my crush shadow or something. She likes the idea of sloppy seconds I guess.

"Truth is gonna look good in platinum, just like his platinum sales!" Bethany gushes.

Dreya rolls her eyes. "Duh. That's the whole reason for the platinum. Platinum sales . . ."

"What about you, Sunday?" Bethany asks. "What are you and your date wearing to prom? Oh, wait. You don't have a date, do you?"

"I have a date, and I will be going to prom, just like I'm actually going to graduate. It's funny how y'all care more about y'all prom colors than a diploma."

"Girl, I don't need a diploma to be a singer!" Dreya says. "Your girl Mystique didn't even graduate."

Dreya and Bethany both crack up laughing like Dreya just told the funniest joke in the world. Whatev. I don't even respond to them, because it's not worth it. Plus, I'm not getting into a shouting match with them when I have to go to the studio later with Mystique and sing my heart out.

My baby cousin Manny marches up from the back bedroom that belongs to me and Dreya. Manny's supposed to share the guest bedroom with his mama, but neither one of them use it. Aunt Charlie mostly sleeps on the couch, and Manny sleeps with me or Dreya. But as soon as Dreya or anybody else tries to actually use their room, Manny and Aunt Charlie have all kinds of conniption fits.

"What are you heffas laughing at?" Manny asks Dreya and Bethany. "Can a brotha get a nap?" Dreya launches a couch pillow at him, which he swiftly dodges. "Ha. That's why you missed, with yo' raggedy self. I'm telling Mommy you was throwing stuff at me and that you and whooty-woot kept me woke."

Bethany sucks her teeth. "What you know about a whooty?"

"I'm five. You would know that if you came to my party. I know you be stretching out the apple on them Apple Bottoms jeans. I don't think it's supposed to be a sideways apple."

OMG! I burst into laughter. I can't hold it in no matter how hard I try. Manny is a trip! Grown one second and whining like a little crybaby the next.

Dreya snatches Manny by the arm and gives him a little whack on his bottom. "Boy, take your grown talkin' self back to bed, 'fore I call Mommy at work."

"She can't even get calls at work. I already tried to call on you. They said it had to be a 'mergency."

"That's *emergency,* you little runt, and you're about to have one," Dreya fusses, "if you don't get back in that bed."

My perpetually unemployed Aunt Charlie has a job right now. She's working at a record store in the mall. She got the job after she told the manager that pop star Drama was her daughter. Dreya didn't want Aunt Charlie working there, but we're not pulling in the big bucks yet, and Aunt Charlie needs money for cigarettes, bingo, and her hair weave.

My phone vibrates on the table, letting me know that I have a new text message.

Be there in five.

I finish up the last paragraph in my English Literature essay. Mystique will be here soon, and I don't want her to have to come in and deal with Dreya and her mini-me Bethany.

Dreya watches me as I put on my high tops and my Aéropostale jacket. She cocks her head to the side, which I have come to know as her nosy look.

"Where are you going?" Dreya asks.

"Out."

"I can see that. Out with who, and where are you going?"

I promptly ignore her and pull on my Juicy Couture

backpack. This is the only expensive thing I've bought with my money. When Sam and I wrote a song for Mystique, we got to split fifty thousand dollars, and I got a fifty thousand dollar advance from Epsilon Records. All of it, except what I spent on this purse, went into my student savings account for my freshman year at Spelman.

Dreya gets up from the couch and walks over to the dining room where I am. "Don't act like you don't hear me, Sunday."

"Back that up, Dreya. You getting me confused with Bethany." I push her out of my way to emphasize that point.

I hear Mystique's car pull up outside, and Bethany's nosy behind runs up to the window to see who it is.

"She's going with Mystique," Bethany announces.

Dreya narrows her eyes that are filled with pure hatred. She can't stand the fact that Mystique has taken me under her wing. Mystique's been in the business for over a decade, and she's only in her late twenties. She's got her own label under Epsilon Records, and I'm one of her debut artists.

Dreya sucks her teeth. "You stay chasing behind Mystique. You ain't nothin' but a groupie to her."

"You and I both know that's not true," I say. "The word you're looking for is protégée. Don't get it twisted."

The doorbell rings, and Bethany lunges for the door to answer it. Mystique never comes to the door any other time, so this is a rare chance for the real groupie to get her shot.

"Hey, Miss Mystique!" Bethany says. For some reason she's adding some extra sista-girl to her tone, like she has to sound black to be down with Mystique. She is so embarrassing.

"Hey ladies, how are y'all doin'?" Mystique's voice is soft and husky with a hint of her Alabama accent still there although she's traveled the world.

Dreya looks Mystique up and down and sashays back over to the couch before answering. "I'm straight."

Her words are soaked with attitude, why I don't know, because even though Mystique is as sweet as pie, she's the kind of person that can make or break you in the industry. Dreya's hating is so out of control that she doesn't even know when she's shooting herself in the foot.

Mystique ignores Dreya's attitude and gives her a syrupy smile. "You havin' a bad day, ma?" she asks.

"Nah," Dreya says with a mean mug expression. "I said I'm straight."

Mystique chuckles and gives Dreya a nonchalant hair flip. "Okay, then. I came in to let you ladies know that my mother wants you to come down to her boutique, Ms. Layla's. She's been designing some pieces for your summer tour, and she's really excited for y'all to see them."

Bethany lets out a half snort, half giggle. I cut my eyes angrily at her. She better not let out another sound. Dreya's giving her the eye too, so she straightens up, and sits down at the dining room table.

Dreya and I have been avoiding our inevitable meeting with Ms. Layla. Her costumes are . . . um . . . unique. She's given Mystique a signature look that includes lots of sparkles, glitter, rhinestones, and sequins. Dreya and I are afraid that she's gonna have us looking like some Mystique copycats on stage.

Mystique lifts a perfectly arched eyebrow. "What's wrong? Y'all aren't saying anything."

"N-nothing's wrong, Mystique," I reply. It is the most unconvincing lie I've ever told.

"Come on, Sunday. I know better. You can be straight with me," Mystique says with the most inviting smile. I don't believe her, though. Mystique and her mama are *tight.*

Dreya says, "Bottom line is, we ain't tryin' to wear none of that stuff your mama has you struttin' around in. I do leather and chains, not sequins. No thanks, and no, ma'am."

Mystique looks at me and laughs. "Sunday, did you think my mother was going to have you in sequins?"

"Is she?" I ask.

"My mother has created stuff that fits each one of you! I've seen some of the costumes, and I think you'll like them. Drama, yours are really edgy, and they match your stage image. Sunday, yours are that preppy hip-hop look you've got going." Mystique puts her arm around me and squeezes, and I feel myself relax.

"No sparkles?" I ask.

"Just a little, tiny bit of sparkle. But I promise you'll like it."

I smile up at Mystique. "I'm trusting you!"

Dreya rolls her eyes. "If I don't like your mama's stuff, I'm hiring a personal stylist to come with me on the road."

Mystique's smile quickly fades and is replaced with a frown. "Actually, you're gonna be using my mother's outfits whether you like it or not. Epsilon Records has contracted her as the sole stylist for the summer tour."

"We'll see about that. Drama doesn't do wack clothes." Dreya crosses her arms in defiance and stares Mystique down.

Mystique laughs out loud. "Save the diva routine. It's not cute, and, sweetie, you aren't even there yet. You'll wear what they tell you, or you'll be sitting at the house. Come on, Sunday. I've got some people I want you to meet, and I'm trying not to be in a bad mood when I get there."

"Okay, I'm ready. Let's roll." I have to bite the inside of my cheek to keep from laughing too.

As we walk out the door, Bethany asks, "Mystique, did your mother design some outfits for me too?"

"What is it that you do again?" Mystique asks with a confused look on her face.

"I'm Dreya's assistant, and I sing backup."

Mystique shrugs. "Oh, okay. Well, I don't think so, but maybe. Come on, Sunday."

On the way to the car, Mystique gives a backward glance to the house. "You and Drama need to drop that other girl. She's gonna be trouble."

"Who, Bethany?" I ask.

Mystique's driver / bodyguard, Benjamin, opens the car door for her and then me. Benjamin, or Benji, as Mystique calls him, doesn't look like the typical big goonie type that would be a bodyguard. He's half-Samoan and half-black and has hair hanging down to the middle of his back, and a pretty boy face. He reminds me of the cover of one of my aunt's romance novels. But his big arms and back and his nearly seven-foot tall body are pretty intimidating.

"Is that her name? She just seems a little extra eager," Mystique replies. "The kind that would do anything for fame."

I nod slowly as I sink into the soft leather of Mystique's custom-made pink Mercedes Benz. She sure did peg Bethany, because she'd do anything right about now to have a record deal and the fab life.

Like Mystique's.

Everything about Mystique's world is fab. She's got the man, the clothes, the cars. As fly as this Benz is, it's Mystique's "play" car—the one she rides in when she goes to the studio or on errands. When she and her man hit the town, it's in a Maybach. They've got the industry and the game on lock.

"We go way back, Mystique. Bethany used to sing with us, so I doubt if Dreya's going to cut her loose."

Mystique gets a faraway look on her face, like she's traveled to another place in her mind. "Sometimes you leave people behind."

We pull into the driveway of a fly mansion in Buckhead. There are a bunch of other cars here too, including Sam's Jeep. The thought of seeing him makes me smile. Then, I see Truth's tricked out Impala and roll my eyes.

"Whose house is this?" I ask Mystique. "Is there a party going on? I thought we were going to the studio."

"Not a party, just some guys hanging out. This is Zachary's Atlanta crib. He's got an artist over who I want you to collaborate with. We'll use Zac's in-house studio. It's the business."

"Your fiancé, Zachary? Zillionaire?"

Mystique chuckles. "Yeah, this is his house. But when

we go inside, don't call him Zillionaire. He hates being called by his rap name. Everybody in his circle just calls him Zac."

"I'm in his circle?" I ask.

"Yeah, Sunday, you are. You're in my circle so you're in his circle."

I'm in Mystique's circle? I'm in Mystique's circle! This is incredible. I wish Dreya could've heard her say that. She would've been heated!

Benji opens up the car door again, and Mystique slides out gracefully. I'm the complete opposite of her, so it's a good thing I'm wearing jeans! As I clumsily stumble out of the car, Benji gives me a flirtatious smile.

Dang, he's fine!

"You better stop looking at me like that!" I fuss. "I'm only eighteen. I'm barely legal."

Benji grins. "Operative word. Legal."

Mystique gives Benji a playful punch on his arm, which probably feels like a mosquito landing on him as strong as he is.

"Benji, leave her alone! You always teasing these young girls," Mystique says.

"I'm just having fun," Benji retorts. "Are you mad, Sunday?"

I shake my head. How can I be mad at him with all that hair rippling over his shoulders, looking like a Black gladiator? Just fine for no reason.

Benji walks us up to the door of Zac's mansion, and before we even go inside I can hear the music bumping.

"I thought you said this wasn't a party," I say.

Mystique laughs out loud. "It's not. Zac just likes to

play his music really, really loud." She pushes the door open and motions for me to follow her inside.

If this isn't a party, I seriously need to check a Webster's Dictionary and get the updated definition. There are little pockets of people dancing, some guys playing Sony PlayStation on a gargantuan flat screen television mounted on a wall, and lots of food.

And there are girls everywhere! I'm talking the video vixen type. Long lace fronts and big booties galore. Truth is posted up on a leather couch with two girls. One of the girls is basically sitting in his lap, and the other has her head resting on his shoulder.

I shake my head and roll my eyes at him. I hope he can see how disgusted I am. Now I see why he didn't come and pick up Dreya today. She's sitting at the house planning their prom outfits, and he's over here creeping.

Mystique pulls my arm and whispers in my ear. "Yeah, that's a mess right there. He's tripping for real."

"Well, if my cousin walked up in here and saw that, she be ready to wreck shop."

Mystique nods. "That's why I didn't invite her. I knew Truth was on some mess, but that's their business. Come and meet Dilly."

"Dilly?"

"Yeah. He's the rapper I want you to collaborate with. He's really good."

We walk through the groups of people and head to the back of the house. Mystique opens a screen door that leads us to a swimming pool, decked out to look like something from the Caribbean. Zac is lounging on a pool chair, and so is Big D. A frown covers my face when I see

LaKeisha, my mom's boyfriend's baby's mama, and her thugged out brother, Bryce, the owner of Club Pyramids.

"What's he doing here?" I whisper to Mystique.

Mystique shrugs. "He's one of Zac's friends, I guess. He owns Club Pyramids."

"I know who he is." My whisper comes out as an angry hiss.

Bryce and his thugs are the ones who stole my college fund. My mother had loaned it to her boyfriend Carlos, when he was trying to buy a stake in their club. Not only did they steal my money, but then they shot Carlos and left him for dead.

After that he disappeared from the hospital, and my mom is still stressing behind it, wondering if Carlos is dead or alive. To say that I can't stand this dude is an understatement. But here he is posted all up in Zac's circle.

Big D rushes over to me, tries to block my view of Bryce. "Hey, baby girl. I didn't know you were coming through."

I look Big D up and down, giving him serious mean mug. "Where's Sam? I saw his Jeep outside."

Big D smiles. "You want to know where your man's at?"

Really, I need Sam to calm me down before I get to blowin' up in Zac's house. Especially since LaKeisha and Bryce have the audacity to keep grinning at me like we're cool or something.

"Why is he here?" I whisper to Big D, knowing he knows who I'm talking about.

Big D turns to Zac, "Let me talk to my artist real quick."

"Hey, Sunday," LaKeisha says as Big D drags me away from the pool and toward the house. "Your single sounds really hot. Looks like you might be going to college after all."

I try to snatch myself out of Big D's arms to lunge at that heifer, but he's . . . well . . . big. I can't budge out of his bear hug.

Mystique, oblivious, of course, to the drama, says, "Her single is hot. It's gonna go to number one on the R & B and Pop charts. No doubt."

Big D whispers in my ear, "Be easy, lil' mama. This isn't the time nor place."

I relax and follow Big D into the house, but I'm still mean mugging him. "Why are they posted up over here?" I ask.

Big D paces back and forth in the chrome-plated kitchen. Everything looks spotless and brand new, as if no one has ever cooked a meal in here. From the looks of the take-out barbeque containers lined up on the shiny counters, no one cooked today.

"Bryce is a club owner, and his little brother is a rapper. Zac always stays in good with them. It's all love between them."

I roll my eyes and deepen my scowl. "Well, it ain't all love between us, and I'm not about to sit up here pretending I like that murderer."

Big D sighs and runs his hand over his low fade. "Come on now, Sunday. You know that stuff don't have nothing to do with you. That's between them and Carlos. Don't mess up your thing with Mystique and Zac behind some 'hood drama."

"Don't you think we owe it to Zac to tell him the kind of dudes he's running with?"

Big D holds a finger up to his lips, giving me the "be quiet" signal. "He knows, but Mystique doesn't. Just chill, okay?"

I take in a huge breath, let it fill up my lungs, and hope that the oxygen will clear my head. Every time I think of what could've happened to Carlos, I want to go swing on Bryce and LaKeisha. Why would LaKeisha even be down with doing something foul to Carlos? He's her daughter's father.

Sam walks into the kitchen reading a text on his phone. "Hey, Sunday, didn't know you were coming. What's poppin', Big D? You need me?"

"Your girl needs you. She's about to burn some serious bridges out there." Big D motions toward the pool area, and Sam peeps out the kitchen window. His gaze stops on Bryce, and he inhales a sharp breath.

"You cool, Sunday? You want me to take you home?" Sam asks.

As much as I do want to flee the scene, I can't. Not without giving Mystique some kind of explanation. And I'm not about to let Bryce or LaKeisha think that they ran me up out of here.

"I can't. Mystique wants me to meet some guy named Dilly. She wants me to collaborate with him on a track."

Big D groans. "Dilly is Bryce and LaKeisha's little brother. He's y'all's age, and has mad flow."

"I'm not collaborating with anybody in that family," I announce.

Sam says, "Don't trip, Sunday. Dilly didn't have anything to do with what happened to Carlos, just like you didn't have anything to do with any dirt Carlos may have done."

My shoulders slump, and I let out a sigh. "All right. I'll be open to it, but I swear if Bryce or LaKeisha say anything wrong to me, I'm blowin' up."

A thin, attractive girl walks into the kitchen with a pouty expression on her lips. She looks like one of those *America's Next Top Model* types. Skinny and waifish enough for high fashion but ethnic enough to look exotic.

"Samuel, what is taking so long? I'm getting lonely in that game room all alone."

My eyes widen. Is this Sam's new boo? His prom date? This party is going from bad to worst-party-EVER!

Sam looks nervously from me to his *friend*. "Uh, Rielle . . . meet Sunday. Sunday, this is Rielle."

Rielle claps her hands together. "You are Sam's artist! The one he's putting on the map!"

Tall tale anyone?

"I'm Sam's artist now?" I ask, not playing into his story at all. Yes, I am hating, and it is well-deserved.

Big D chuckles. "Well, you're one of many that he's working with. You know what he means."

Rielle giggles and says, "I think it's so cute that he's taking you to your prom. Producer and protégée. The blogs will love it."

I shake my head angrily. "Okay, I don't know what he's been telling you, but . . ."

Before I can finish my put-Sam-on-blast tirade, Mystique glides into the kitchen. She opens a cooler on the counter and pulls out a soda. "You ready to meet Dilly?" she asks. "He's excited about working with you."

I narrow my eyes at Sam, and decide to burst his bubble later. "Sure, Mystique. Let's do the do, but can we go into Zac's studio? The sun is beaming extra hard out there, and it was making me a little lightheaded."

"Sure. Big D, can you show her where the studio is? I'll go get Dilly, and we'll meet y'all in there."

Mystique takes her soda back out toward the pool area, and Big D leads me down a long corridor. I make a backward glance at Sam and give him an extra evil glare.

"Sam didn't mean for you to find out about Rielle," Big D says. "She's nobody. Just a prom date."

I don't respond, because I can't stand when guys stick up for each other like that. First of all, if she was only a prom date, then what is she doing here at Zac's mansion? Sounds like more than prom to me. And second, if she wasn't important then why did Sam go out of his way lying and making up stories trying to seem like he's important.

"I thought you told me he would get over all the fight with Truth," I say to Big D. "You were wrong."

Big D replies, "I wasn't wrong. He did get over it. I didn't think he'd moved on to the next chick, though."

"Well, thank you for being so encouraging. Thanks a lot."

Big D slings his gigantic arm around my shoulder. "I'm just keeping it one hundred with you, girl. It would do you much better to get over Sam too. That way we can have peace on our tour."

"So you trying to tell me you don't want any drama when Sam pushes up on groupies?"

"I'm saying Sam has moved on, and you should too."

Big D pushes open a huge double door that leads to Zac's studio. This spot is totally decked out. The sound board is like twice the size of Big D's, and the recording room has enough space for a whole gospel choir. It's crazy how he's got this set up in his house! And he doesn't even live in Atlanta. I wonder what his New York studio looks like.

"Are you impressed?" Mystique's voice floats over to me like a feather on the wind. Sounds poetic doesn't it?

I turn to answer her, but my voice gets caught in my throat. The boy that's with her, I'm assuming that he's Dilly, has just the right amount of fineness to help me get over Sam. He's what we call bright, down here in ATL, a black boy with light skin. His hair is cut low, and has deep waves. His eyes are big and pretty, with long lashes touching the sky. Hotness personified.

He reaches his hand out to me. For a half second I don't know what he wants, then I realize he wants me to shake hands with him.

"I'm Jayson, but you can call me Dilly. You're Sunday?"

I nod, trying not to get lost in his eyes. "Pleased to meet you."

"I heard your single. Mystique let me listen. It's good."

"Thank you."

Okay, I don't think I've ever been this polite in my life. But I can't think of anything else to say. Because what do you say to the younger brother of the thug who tried to kill your mother's boyfriend and almost stepdaddy? I mean, do I say, "So pleased to make your acquaintance?" Come the heck on! He's related to LaKeisha and Bryce. I can't help but dead all thoughts of a potential crush even though he is ridiculously fine.

Mystique cuts in. "So, I want y'all to hear this track that Zac did, and tell me if you think you can groove to it."

She trots over to the sound boards and presses a few buttons. I'm impressed that she knows her way around a studio. I've got to get that piece under my belt too, since Sam is acting up.

The track is not what I'm used to, but still I think I can work with it. Mostly drums and bass, but not a lot of melody.

I bob my head a little, sway back and forth to the sound of the drumbeat. Then, Dilly starts a freestyle verse.

"Every time I go round / She tellin' me to slow down / Actin' like I'm low down / No matter how my flow sound / He's a clown / that other dude she flossin' / Cookies he'll be tossin' / When they let the boss in / I'ma win / Never lose 'cause I'm a winner / I eat emcees with collard greens fo' my dinner."

Big D and Mystique clap when he's done, but I just lift one of my eyebrows and give him an up and down glance. It was aiight. He's got a little bit of lyrical swiftness, but he could use some polish.

"What did you think?" Dilly asks me.

"You're good," I say. "Am I supposed to rap on this too, or y'all just want me singing the hook?"

Big D lets out a huge laugh. "This girl is all about her business, know what I mean?"

"I'm just saying! Trying to figure out what I have to do."

Honestly, I'm not feeling anywhere close to creative right now. I'm stressed beyond belief, and the muse is definitely not in the building. My mind keeps going back to Sam and Rielle all booed up.

Mystique says, "You can do whatever you want to the track. I'm gonna give you both an MP3 of it and see what y'all come up with. We can have a jam session next weekend."

"You cool with that, Sunday?" Dilly asks, as if all of this hinges on my participation.

"Sure."

Now that I've agreed to this collaboration, I'm ready to go home. I need to listen to sad breakup songs, and cry into my pillow. And all of this needs to happen with a quickness.

How is it that I finally figure out that I'm digging Sam after he's already moved on? Looks like it's over between us, before it even started.

3

Hours after our miniature studio session I get home from Zac's party. Mystique meant to have Benji take me home right after my mini-session with Dilly, but then got sidetracked by someone Zac wanted her to meet. She didn't get back to me until much later, and I had to endure two more hours of watching Sam push up on Rielle and Truth push up on groupies. Not exactly my idea of how to spend a Friday night, know what I mean?

I slam the front door as I walk in. This causes Aunt Charlie to jerk to an upright position on the couch where she was napping. A thin plume of smoke rises from the cigarette in the ashtray in front of her. One day she's going to burn our house down. I pour her leftover soda over the cigarette and frown as it floats in the Pepsi.

"Dreya's not with you?"

I shake my head. "Naw. I went out with Mystique."

Aunt Charlie frowns, and scratches underneath her wig. "Mystique? Why she ain't take Dreya too? Was this some kind of publicity thing?"

Aunt Charlie has been heated ever since I signed a record deal of my own. She accused me of trying to steal Dreya's shine, even though I'm the whole reason for Dreya's having a record deal too. If I hadn't written that fly hook for Truth's album, no one would even know about her.

"No, it wasn't a publicity thing," I reply. "It was a get together for some of her fiancé's friends."

"Well, next time, you could ask Dreya if she wants to go."

"How do I look inviting Dreya to someone else's house? If Mystique had wanted Dreya there, she would've invited her."

"You need to stand up for your cousin. Y'all are family."

I roll my eyes and walk down the hallway to my bedroom. Aunt Charlie acts like this is kindergarten when Dreya got to go anywhere I was invited. I remember once I got invited to Chuck E. Cheese's, and Aunt Charlie dropped us both off, and didn't come back until hours after the party was supposed to be over. She went to get her hair and nails done while we were at the party. My mother was so mad.

My phone rings. It's Sam. I press Ignore. Not even trying to hear anything from him right now.

I slam my bedroom door behind me and peel off my clothes. I consider taking a shower, but that would require me to go back out there and listen to more non-sense about Tolliver solidarity from Aunt Charlie. I vote no.

Instead of pajamas, I tug on an oversized *That's So Raven* sleep shirt that my mom bought me a few years ago for Christmas. It is my most comfortable shirt—flaws and all.

My lumpy, bumpy, seven-year-old mattress is the pits, but I'm too tired to be bothered by it. I need to skim a little bit of my royalty money and get a Sealy Posturepedic up in the spot. But if I do, it will probably be my little cousin's favorite place to take a nap, which means it'll be covered in pee stains. I'll wait until I've got my own spot.

As soon as I close my eyes and start drifting to dreamland, I hear a loud tap on my window. I sit straight up in my bed and pull my comforter over me, even though it's warm in my room. That better not be Sam, because I'm gonna get all kinds of ugly if he's waking me up to explain his groupie escapades.

I hear the tapping again and sigh. I'm really going to have to see who it is. I reach on the nightstand for my cell phone and dial 9 then 1. I swear if it's somebody crazy, I'm pressing the other 1 and then hightailing my little self to the front of the house.

My mouth drops open when I see who it is at my window.

"Sunday! It's me. Open up."

It's my mother's missing boyfriend, Carlos.

I shake my head, not knowing whether I should open the window or not. For a half second I wonder if he's a ghost or something, because the last we heard he was maybe dead.

"Come on, *niña*. Someone might see me. It's cool."

"Go to the front door," I whisper, but he can't hear me through the glass.

He shakes his head and shrugs, and I point toward the front of the house.

"No! I don't want Charlie to see me. Plus, they're watching the house."

Now I throw the window open. "Who's watching the house?"

Carlos climbs through the window. He's wearing a black T-shirt and army fatigue pants. His long hair is pulled back into a ponytail, and he looks tired.

"Bryce and LaKeisha. They've got people driving by every night. Seeing if they can spot me."

Finally, the shock wears off, and I throw my arms around his neck. Then I punch him in the arm. "Fool! My mama thought you were dead. She's gonna beat the mess outta you."

"I hope not," he chuckles. "I'm not all the way healed yet."

"What's still wrong with you?"

"One of those bullets punctured my lung. It's hard for me to breathe now. I breathe like an eighty-year-old man who smoked cigarettes his entire life."

"For real? That's messed up."

"Is Shawn here?"

I nod. "It's late, so she's probably in her room asleep. Are you sure you want me to wake her up?"

Carlos runs his hand over his head and paces the floor. "Sunday, I've been in town a week figuring out how I'm gonna see my Shawn. She's gonna hate me, but I love her so much. I've gotta see her before I leave town again."

"Okay. I'll get her."

I tiptoe out of my bedroom, to my mother's room. I quietly open the door to my mom's room, as if Aunt Charlie could hear me—she's got *Dreamgirls* blasting on the television, and she's trying to sing along with Jennifer Hudson. The sound is not a pleasing one.

My mother is sleeping so peacefully that I hate to wake her. Especially to this mess here, because she's about to trip the heck out.

"Ma, wake up," I whisper as I gently shake her body.

"W-what is it, Sunday?"

"It's Carlos . . ."

She bolts upright. "Did they find him?"

"No. He found us. He's in my room. Just climbed in the window."

I hold a finger up to my mouth to shush any other squealing my mom wants to do. I can tell she has a thousand questions, which she might as well hold onto. I don't have any answers.

We both creep back to my bedroom. My mother stands still for a moment—staring at Carlos. Neither of them say a word; they just stare and breathe. My mother's breaths sound clear and even, Carlos's sound weak and rattled.

Then, my mother lunges toward Carlos and lands in his arms. She hugs him like she's clinging for dear life, and I can hear the sobs that she tries to muffle by putting her face in his chest. He hugs her back, and tears trail down his face as well.

"Shawn, I . . ." Carlos starts to speak.

"Don't say anything yet!" my mother exclaims. "Let me just look at you."

My mother pulls away from him and looks him up and down. She strokes his face, runs her finger over the bullet wound on his neck, and then takes one of his hands.

"It's a miracle that you're here, baby," my mother says. "I thought you were gone."

"I would've been if it hadn't been for my family in Brooklyn."

"Brooklyn? You're in New York now?"

"Yes, I'm in New York with my cousins."

"Just like that? Why haven't you called?"

Carlos sighs and throws his head back. "I thought it would be easier for you if I disappeared. My cousins aren't good guys, Shawn. They aren't people you'd want to deal with."

"They're thugs like Bryce, then," my mother says with a frown.

"Worse. But they were the only option. We didn't have any money."

"Are you back in Atlanta for good?" she asks.

"No. I'm leaving tonight. I just wanted to see you. To let you know I'm alive."

"Well, what good is that, if you're not here?"

Carlos shrugs. "It's all I've got right now. But soon, we won't have to worry about Bryce or any of those dudes down at Club Pyramids. I promise you that."

"What are you going to do?" my mother asks. I can hear the fear in her tone.

"Don't worry about it. I'm going to make everything up to you and Sunday."

Carlos grabs my mother into his arms and kisses her. I watch her go limp in his embrace. When he finally lets her go, he has tears in his eyes again.

"I've got to go, Shawn. I'm putting you in danger by being here."

"Can't you leave in the morning?" my mother pleads.

Carlos shakes his head and lifts my window. "Sunday," he says. "I'm going to get your college money back."

"Don't worry about that. I've got it covered." I can't believe these words are coming out of my mouth. Maybe I'm getting all emotional because he's here.

Carlos climbs backwards out of my window as my mother stands looking helpless with her hand over her mouth. As soon as I close the window she breaks down crying. I don't know how to comfort her. I can't think of one thing to say that might make her feel better.

"At least he's alive."

While this is a true statement, it doesn't stop my mother's tears from falling. I wish we could go back in time to before the shooting. Back to when Carlos was slumming on our couch because my mom wouldn't let him in her bedroom without a ring. Back to when I didn't have to worry about having a crush on a new somebody because he might just be related to an attempted murderer.

Can somebody loan me a time machine?

4

_____

First thing in the morning, my mom told Aunt Charlie about her visit from Carlos. I didn't think it was a good idea to tell her, but my mom and her sister are best friends. No matter how much Aunt Charlie gets on my nerves, I know she'd never do anything to hurt my mom.

They decided to take Manny to the zoo, to get my mother's mind off of it, although it probably won't work. But at least she'll be out of the house, and she won't be walking around crying all day.

I've got the house to myself, because Dreya's at Big D's house—where she's been since last night. Today, she's supposed to be doing studio remixes of some of her album tracks. What will I do with my peace and quiet?

My phone buzzes in my pocket. I just got a text message.

I'm outside. U gonna let me in?

Okay, clearly I'm not going to have any peace and quiet, because Sam picks now, of all times, to drop by. And who does he think he is anyway, dropping by? I shouldn't let him in, but I peek out the door and see his smiling face.

"Come in," I say with attitude, as I swing the door open.

Sam chuckles, "I feel so welcome."

"You do? Dang. I was going for the exact opposite of that."

Sam perches on the arm of the couch and gives me a goofy grin. "I know you're mad about Rielle. That's why I'm here."

"Why would you think I'm mad?" I sit down on the love seat and give him a confused look as if what he's saying is completely ludicrous.

"Come on, Sunday. You were about to explode on me over Zac's house."

"Nope. Wasn't about to do anything like that. What I look like blowin' up over somebody else's dude?"

"Well, even if you won't admit that you're mad, I'm here to apologize. Rielle is not, nor has she ever been, nor will she ever be anything other than a date. She's going to prom with me, and I mentioned the thing at Zac's house while we were picking out corsages."

I roll my eyes. Why does he think I want to hear about his prom plans?

"Speaking of which," he continues, "what color is your dress? Do I need to get a matching vest or anything for my tux?"

Dang. Why did I ask him to go to prom with me? Bad idea.

"You know what? I think I'm gonna skip it," I say. "Prom is for suckas anyway."

Sam laughs out loud. "Are you serious? You just asked me like five minutes ago."

"And now I'm un-asking you."

"And this has nothing to do with Rielle?"

"It has nada to do with Rielle."

Sam pokes his lips out with a "yeah right" expression. I wish he would stop, because them soup coolers are already large enough without him adding anything extra.

"Did you get a dress?" he asks.

I sigh. "Why does it matter? Didn't I just say I was skipping it?"

A tiny smile graces Sam's lips. I can't stand him, because he looks so cute right now. Grrr!

"I want to see it."

"What? The dress?"

Sam folds his arms and nods as if he's not leaving my couch until he sees my prom dress. I storm back to my room, snatch the shimmery, short green dress out of my closet and lay it on the couch.

"See, there it is."

"I bet that looks hot on you," Sam says.

"Yeah, it does."

"So can you model it?" Sam asks.

I narrow my eyes angrily. I don't know who this dude thinks he is, but his swagger ain't all like that, where he's gonna parade some other chick in my face and still think we're cool. I don't even think so.

"No, Sam. I cannot model it, because I will be returning it to the store."

Sam hops down off the couch, tilts his head to one side, and sighs. "Sunday, don't wreck your prom trying to get back at me. It only happens once."

"It's cool, Sam. I don't really want to go."

He looks at me like he doesn't believe me, and it's probably because I'm not convincing. Shoot, I don't even believe myself. But there is no way in the world that I am going anywhere with him after he goes to prom with that Rielle girl.

I'm much too fly for another girl's leftovers.

"So are you ready for Drama's single to come out?"

Sam's talking about the first song that he and I wrote for Dreya. It's called "Love Is." Just the mention of the song takes me back into the studio where we vibed really tough all day and night. We wrote Dreya's entire album in one weekend, and I think that's where the crush-like feelings began.

Well, *Sam's* crush started then, but I wasn't really on it at that time. If I had been, we'd be all boyfriended and girlfriended up right about now. Now all I've got is suspicions of him being lip-locked with a chicken named Rielle.

"I'm ready for the single to drop, because I'm ready to make number one and get this paper," I say.

Sam leans on the wall, getting all comfortable again. I thought he was about to go home. I feel myself sigh out of bugaboo weariness. I'm so ready for him to go on somewhere. I'd like to go wallow in my dateless prom sorrow.

"That's still all you care about?" he asks. "How about people hearing your music and thinking it's fresh?"

I open my eyes wide and nod, like I'm thinking "duh!" "When people hear my music and think it's fresh, they cop the ringtone and the MP3."

"Too bad we aren't collecting royalties."

I frown. "Yeah, I shouldn't have let you and Big D talk me out of all my rights for a piddly thousand dollars a song. But it's whatever. Every song I write for my album, I'm getting paid in full."

"We need to put in some more work on your record. When are you coming to the lab for an all-nighter?"

I shrug. "Maybe after prom, graduation, and all that."

"I love your enthusiasm, Sunday. I get all excited just talking to you."

His sarcasm is evident. But how does he expect me to be enthusiastic about being holed up in a room with him for twenty-four hours or more? He must have me confused with Rielle.

"You know what, Sam? I think you should just go now, before I say something that you'll regret."

Sam laughs out loud. "Always the tough one, right? You're gonna have to let somebody in one day."

"Maybe you're right. But that day ain't today."

I walk Sam to the door and open it wide. I'm ready to get back to my peaceful, quiet afternoon. Maybe I'll fantasize about walking across the stage at graduation or maybe I'll dream about my first day on Spelman's campus.

I can tell you what I won't be daydreaming about— Sam and his raggedy, chicken prom date.

5

It is now, officially, the Saturday before prom and I still don't have a date. Not that I'm looking for one, but I'm just saying. I'm dateless for senior prom, but maybe I'm hoping because I haven't taken the dress back, nor have I gotten rid of my prom and after prom tickets.

But what am I hoping for?

Definitely not for Sam to kick Rielle to the curb. I wouldn't go with him now if someone paid me. Well . . . maybe I would, if someone paid enough, but bottom line is no one is paying me to go to prom with Mr. Swagger America.

So maybe I'm not hoping for anything.

What I definitely am doing is chilling at Big D's studio. Dilly and I just had a ridiculous jam session! I came with my A game, because he got his little flow on at Zac's house, and I was too stressed to display anything I had.

He was impressed with my rhyming and singing skills, and the feeling was mutual. Dilly is super talented himself. I'm trying to figure out if he's a foster kid or something, because he's just too cool to be related to LaKeisha and Bryce.

Dilly takes a huge swig from his bottle of water. His eyes close while he guzzles, and those long, dark eyelashes brush against his cheek. He's got little pieces of fruit floating in his water bottle, kind of a girly thing to do, I think. Even though he's hot, I actually subtracted swag points for the strawberries in the water.

"You are so lucky to be working with Mystique," Dilly says. "My album has been on hold forever, but your stuff will be out soon."

"Is that because of Mystique?" I ask, not exactly sure what he's getting at.

"Heck yeah. Zac's label has like fifty artists all trying to put out albums. And everybody just can't come out at the same time."

"And that's holding you back?"

"Yeah, like there's not enough promo money for everyone to come out at the same time, so we gotta wait. I'm like last in line."

I guess this makes sense. "But can you get moved up in line? What if Zac thinks you've got something really hot?"

Dilly grins. "Yeah, that's why I'm hoping you'll collaborate with me. You're what's up right now."

"Nah, Dreya and Truth are what's up. They're still trying to figure out what to do with me."

Dilly shakes his head. "You are like a quadruple threat, ma. You've got to know that. Drama won't be around for a long time, but you will."

"That's what they keep telling me. But enough shop talk. Tell me something about you."

He shrugs and gives me that sweet grin again. "Like what?"

"Tell me how you came up with Dilly for a rap name?"

"Girls always be calling me silly when I'm tryin' to holla. They be like, you so silly! So I just picked something that rhymed."

I get tickled, even though I don't want to. I don't really want to like this guy. I keep remembering who he calls family. It's not hard to hate them, but it's getting really hard to hate Dilly.

As if he's reading my thoughts he says, "Listen, I know you're feeling some kind of way about working with me. I get it. I would feel crazy about this too."

"So you're saying your brother and sister really did have Carlos shot?"

He throws both hands up. "Naw. I ain't sayin' that. But I know that's what you think."

"So what *are* you saying? Because for real, helping you blow up means helping them blow up, and I can't sleep at night if I'm giving a hookup to Bryce."

Not to mention that chump still has my college tuition money. But I'm not going there with Dilly. They're already way too deep in my mix.

"What I'm saying is, Carlos isn't all that innocent."

"You saying he had that coming to him?"

Now this dude is about to really make me mad. I know

that everything Carlos does isn't necessarily on the up and up, but he's good to my mother, and just a good person all around. He's not the villain of this story.

"I'm not saying he had it coming to him, but I know for a fact, he's done some dirt."

We sit quietly for a moment, while I let this sink in. I've never thought Carlos was a saint, but for him to be dirty like Bryce and them? I can't see it.

"Can we just not let their drama have anything to do with us?"

"Like the Montagues and the Capulets?"

Dilly nods and smiles. "Exactly like them. You like Shakespeare?"

"*Romeo and Juliet*. Required reading, dude," I say with a chuckle. "I'm more into contemporary African American writers."

"Gotcha. But, for real, I don't care about the beef our families have. I think you've got mad vocal skills, and your lyrics are fiyah. I want to work with you."

"You got skills too, boy. I ain't gonna lie."

"So let's do this."

His cuteness has just inspired me to ask him something that I'll probably regret, but I'm doing it anyway.

"Do you want to go to prom with me? I know it's last minute, but I'm dateless."

Dilly's eyes widen with what looks like shock. "A hottie like you? Dateless for prom? That's messed all the way up."

"It's a long story. You down or what?"

"I'm only a junior. Is that okay?"

"Yeah, that's cool."

"You a cougar?" Dilly cracks up.

"Right. I'm a cougar! Boy, I'm wearing green, so find yourself something that matches."

"I can do that."

For a long moment, Dilly and I stare at each other as if we're waiting on birds to sing or something. What I see on his face is innocence, I think. Did I mention that it's really hard for me to hate him?

Our moment is interrupted by Big D, Truth, Dreya, Sam, and Bethany, who burst into the studio room completely uninvited. And noisy too. Just rude.

"Here y'all are," Big D says. "We're waiting on y'all so we can have our summer tour meeting."

I watch as Sam narrows his eyes and glares at Dilly. I hope he doesn't think he's got anything to say about anything! I'm not his chick.

"We weren't hiding," I reply. "Are we gonna meet down here?"

Truth says, "We don't need Dilly for this, though. Were y'all finished?"

"Actually, he can stay," Big D says. "He's not going on tour with us, but he needs to hear this news from BET."

Truth looks twisted, but straddles one of the keyboard benches. Bethany and Dreya move across the room together, like Dreya's on a catwalk and Bethany's her shadow. They even sit down on the leather couch like two synchronized swimmers. The only difference I see is that Bethany is beaming over at Dilly. Dreya's looking all nonchalant like she wishes the meeting was over already.

Sam chooses to stand I guess, because he puts his back against the wall and posts up. He gives me a little head nod, and I return the gesture. There's all kinds of tension up in this spot, and none of it is coming from me or Dilly. We're cool as what.

Big D says, "Y'all should be pumped at how excited BET is about this reality show. Since Sam and Truth's fight video on YouTube is up to a hundred thousand hits, they upped the number of episodes."

Truth grins and shakes his locs out of his face. "That's what's up," he says.

"Now they want to do a countdown to the tour special," Big D continues. "They want to follow y'all around in the weeks before the tour. We've set it up so that the cameras can come into the costume fitting at Ms. Layla's boutique. They're also going to hang around here at the studio for rehearsals, and they're sending a camera crew with y'all to prom."

Sam lifts an eyebrow. "You going, Sunday? If it's gonna be on BET then you have to go."

"I don't have to do anything I don't want to do," I reply, "but it just so happens that I am going to prom. Just not with you."

Big D laughs. "Hey y'all, save it for the cameras!"

Bethany says, "I don't know if my dress is fly enough for TV! I might have to pick something else out."

"As long as you don't try to pick something platinum. That's my color," Dreya says, with a strong dose of evil side eye to let Bethany know she's serious.

"We should all go in the same limo," Truth suggests. "And have the cameras posted up on the inside."

"I thought we were renting a Lambo!" Dreya whines. "I can't be seen going to prom in an average limo."

Big D frowns. "Everyone can fit in a limo, including the BET cameras that they plan to mount on the ceiling. That ain't going down in a Lambo."

Dreya shrugs and asks, "But isn't it going to be weird with Sunday not having a date?"

"She has a date," Dilly says. "I'm going with her."

Truth frowns. "Then dead what I said about us all riding together. I can't be seen chilling with the competition."

So Truth is looking at Dilly like he's competition? Wow. We're all on the same record label, so shouldn't they be like partners?

"I can't touch you right now, Truth. It's all you," Dilly says.

I can't tell if Dilly is being sincere or if he's just stroking Truth's massive ego. Me personally, I think that Dilly can rap circles around Truth. But since nobody is asking me, I'm not bringing up my opinion on the matter.

Big D nods. "Listen, the limo thing is a good idea. I like it, and Dilly can roll too. But before y'all start planning a little prom night spree, let me give y'all the scoop from Epsilon Records. No underage drinking. Not champagne, not a wine cooler, nothing. No cussing. No hooking up on camera."

Truth laughs out loud. "Then what am I gonna be doing? You just took out my major activities."

Big D glares at Truth. "I'm not kidding on the underage stuff. Until you're twenty-one, I better not see you drinking."

"You ain't my daddy!" Truth blurts, and then cracks up laughing.

"Epsilon Records has sponsors for the tour, and they're more worried about them than your swagger, so keep it clean," Big D says.

"Not trying to be funny," Dreya says, "but isn't this gonna be a boring reality show?"

"It doesn't have to be. Just be yourselves when the cameras are rolling," Big D advises. "Dreya, Sunday, and Bethany, Mystique will be here soon to pick y'all up to go to Ms. Layla's boutique."

"So we're going to start filming our reality show *to-night?*" I ask.

My hand self-consciously goes to the high ponytail on the top of my head. I mean, I look cute with a round-the-way-girl kinda swag, but this look is definitely not made for TV.

Big D says, "Yes, tonight. It's gonna go quickly. We'll be filming the countdown to the tour show for two weeks, and then we'll film the entire six-week summer tour. BET will stretch it out and make it last the whole fall TV season."

"They're gonna be at graduation too?" Dreya asks.

"Yeah. Are you graduating?" Big D asks.

This is a very valid question. Last time I heard, Dreya had a solid D+ average, and was ranked in the bottom five percent of our class. The only people below her were the juvenile delinquents. Even the kids in special education outranked Dreya.

Dreya gives Big D the hand. "Yeah, I'm graduating. All of my teachers signed my final grades."

Truth walks over to where Dreya is sitting, throws his

arm around Dreya's neck and pulls her close. He kisses her on the neck and says, "That's what's up, baby."

"For real? Aunt Charlie is gonna be pumped," I say. "Congratulations, Dreya. I didn't think you were gonna make it."

"Shut up, Sunday. Don't try to act like I'm stupid. I don't do well in school, but it's by choice. I'm not stupid." Dreya rolls her eyes and pouts like I've really hurt her feelings.

I blink about one hundred times while giving her my tight-lipped stare. Not doing well in school on *purpose*. Isn't that the definition of stupid? She said it, not me.

Big D stands up from his wooden stool and stretches like he's been working on the railroad somewhere. "One more thing, y'all. This is really important. Don't ever, ever, make any reference to the cameras while you're filming. You can only look into the camera when they do those confessional things."

"So we pretend that the camera isn't there? Isn't there gonna be like a whole crew?" Bethany asks. "The camera loves me, so how am I supposed to just ignore it?"

Can somebody please ice this chick? I mean, really. Too absurd that she has a comment about this reality show. She's lucky to even be on there.

"Bethany, you better not say anything stupid on camera, or you're off the show," Dreya says. "And yeah, I can fire you, because you're only doing this because you're my personal assistant. Speaking of which, can you fetch me a beverage? My throat is parched."

Everyone looks from Bethany to Dreya and back to Bethany. I'm wondering if she's ever going to stand up for herself! Dreya wouldn't get out on me like that. I wouldn't care how many record deals she had. She's clowning for real.

Big D says, "You need to stop with that diva act, Drama. She ain't on the clock right now."

"Why I gotta be acting like a diva?" Dreya asks. "I'm thirsty for real. She's supposed to be my assistant."

Bethany stands up from the couch. "It's cool. I'll get it. You want Sprite, right?"

"Yeah."

Bethany starts to walk away, but then she turns to Dreya and asks, "Don't you have anything else to say?"

I cover my mouth to keep from giggling. If she's waiting for Dreya to say the magic word, she's gonna be standing there until the end of days.

Dreya bites her lip as if she's thinking really hard. Then as if the light finally went on in her brain, her eyes widen, and she smiles.

"You're right," she says. "Make sure you put it in a tall glass with ice."

Dreya pulls out her iPhone and starts texting or whatever she's doing, like she didn't just treat Bethany like her name was Kunta Kinte.

Bethany narrows her eyes into little slits and glares at Dreya, like if she wasn't trying to get a record deal herself, she'd be smacking Dreya all upside her head. I really wish she would, because that would be super funny. And the best part is that Dreya would fire her if she did that, and then I wouldn't have to see her backstabbing face every time I turn around.

Big D frowns at Dreya too, and shakes his head. "Truth,

Dilly, Sam, it's a wrap. Y'all can hang if y'all want to, but I've got to take Shelly to a concert."

"Look at you, Big D," Bethany purrs on her way out of the room. "Taking your lady out like a true don is supposed to. I wish I had a man like you."

"So thirsty! Girl, you need to quit," Dreya says. "He's old enough to be your daddy or something."

"It's not like I want him!" Bethany says. "I just want someone like him."

Dilly stands. "Can I get a ride home, D?"

"Shelly is waiting for me. Sam, can you take care of that for me? Drop him over Bryce's house."

Sam lifts an eyebrow and smiles at me. "Sure, come on, Dilly. Let's blow this popsicle stand."

Bethany sucks her teeth. "So corny."

"But you want me, though," Sam quips back.

Dreya rolls her eyes. "Why don't y'all get together already?"

Sam looks at me, I guess trying to get my reaction. But I don't have one. If he wants to kick it with Rielle, Bethany, or whoever, it's all good. As long as it doesn't affect my beats or my cash. Know what I mean?

"Let's bounce up out of here, Dilly, before somebody gets her feelings hurt," Sam says.

Feelings hurt? Whatever. He should've checked that before he brought Rielle all up in the spot. From the twisted look on his face as he turns to leave, I'm thinking the only one catching hurt feelings is Sam.

6

I take one look at myself in the mirror of Ms. Layla's boutique, wearing a one-piece denim bodysuit with leather patches on the knees, black ankle boots, and hoop earrings. I've got a fake smile on my face, but I'm screaming on the inside.

I can't. I just can't.

I thought Mystique said that her mama was going to make me personalized outfits. Like something I would actually want to wear. She's gonna have me looking like a hot, ghetto, ratched mess.

And why are Dreya and Bethany standing over there snickering? Wait until it's Dreya's turn. If this is what they gave me, I know hers is gonna be crazy, because she's supposed to be the "edgy" one.

Mystique asks, "So, what do you think?"

She's got this big expectant smile on her face, *and* the BET cameras are rolling. How can I tell the truth?

"What do I think?" I ask. I'm trying to stall for time so that I can come up with something believable.

Thinking . . . thinking . . . Yeah, I got nothing.

"Do you like the outfit?" she asks again.

I look around to see if Ms. Layla is coming back into the room. She ran in the back of her shop to fix a hem in a pair of pants.

"There are some things about it that I like," I say after a really long pause. You would think that after all that stalling, I would've come up with something better.

Dreya bursts into laughter. "Like what?" she asks. "Is it the knee patches? Because that's my favorite part of the outfit."

"Mine too," giggles Bethany. "No wait. My favorite part is the hungry butt."

And by "hungry butt" she means the fact that this bodysuit is all up in my behind. A denim wedgie.

I spin around and give them both an angry glare. "Shut up! It's a stage costume."

"That's right," Mystique says. "It's not supposed to look like something you'd normally wear."

Right. Like who would wear a sleeveless blue jean bodysuit? Ever? Did I forget to mention that it was sleeveless? Welcome to my nightmare.

Ms. Layla walks up from the back of the store and grimaces. "What are you wearing, Sunday?"

I lift my eyebrows! This is exactly the question I want to ask her. *What* in the world am I wearing?

I look down at the outfit. "This is the one your assistant gave me to try on."

"No, no. That one is for Drama. All of the bodysuits are for her. Your stuff is less edgy and more regular teen."

I close my eyes and let out a huge sigh of relief. After trying on this ratchedness, I'll take regular teen any day.

Dreya leans back and gives her most exaggerated neck roll. "I don't care if you are Mystique's mama. I am *not* wearing that!"

Did this heifer forget that the cameras are on and that Mystique and her unfabulous mama can make or break her career? Or maybe she forgot that Mystique is a platinum-selling recording artist, and the only reason why a lot of people will tune into this show is because she's on it. Maybe she forgot that her own first single hasn't even come out yet, and that a project can be yanked and shelved without any explanation whatsoever.

Yeah, she's got a real case of amnesia up in this piece. She better find a cure quick, or she's gonna be filling out applications for a summer job at Sonic.

"Well, what exactly is it that you want to wear, Drama?" Ms. Layla asks, classy as ever. Not one neck roll or finger-snap. If this was Aunt Charlie, there'd be all kinds of hair weave flying right about now.

Dreya is caught completely off guard, I think, and left without a comeback. She's used to people sparring with her, but Ms. Layla is not about to do that. Neither she nor Mystique seem much like the brawling type.

"I think she would look good in skinny jeans and leather accessories," Bethany offers, trying to save her friend. "Like a leather choker with spikes on it and leather belts wrapped around her waist and legs."

Dreya high-fives Bethany. "My girl! That's what I'm talking about. Something hot to death that's gonna make them dudes go crazy."

Bethany must have already forgotten how a couple of hours ago, she was Dreya's slave girl. Now they're besties again. They're special. And not the kind of special you say when you do something nice for someone, as in, "I baked you a special treat." No. These two are special in a mildly medicated kind of way.

Ms. Layla looks as if she's considering Bethany's suggestion. With one hand she smoothes the side of her honey blond lace front wig, and with the other hand she taps her chin. Then, something suddenly strikes her as funny. She reaches over and grabs one of her hip-hop magazines off of the coffee table and turns to a specific page. She hands the magazine to Dreya.

"You mean something like this?"

Even though I'm dying to take off this cooter cuttin' bodysuit, I need to see this photo. I look over Dreya's shoulder, as does Bethany on the other side. The picture is of another R & B chick, Hot Chocolate. She's wearing almost exactly what Bethany described.

Can somebody say "epic fail"? No R & B diva would be caught dead rocking a similar outfit to her competition.

"You 'bout to have me looking like a swagger jacker!" Dreya fusses. "Next time you think you have an idea, tell yourself never mind."

Bethany gets a wounded expression on her face. As a matter of fact her face is on the floor waiting to be picked up and put back on. Ms. Layla examines her perfectly done French manicure as if she couldn't care less.

"I was just trying to help," Bethany mumbles.

"If you two are done, we can discuss some different options for Drama," Ms. Layla says. "The outfits I'm showing you are examples. You're free to choose whatever you want from the collection."

"I'm going to take this off now," I say, tired of my butt's being attacked by this fabric.

Ms. Layla replies, "Go ahead to the back room, and my assistant will give you both more suitable outfits to model."

Dreya and I both hurry toward the changing room. The BET television audience will already have more than enough views of my behind in this monstrosity.

The assistant hands me a highly appropriate pair of khaki cargo carpri pants, a fitted tiny tee, and a jeweled and bedazzled half jean jacket. I will look past the rainbow of rhinestones, because anything is better than what I'm wearing now.

Dreya's costume looks like something one of the crew of the Starship Enterprise would wear. It's an all-silver catsuit with a wide zipper down the front. When the assistant helped Dreya into it, she zipped it all the way up.

Hello. Has she met Dreya?

Dreya promptly zipped it halfway down so that her miniature breast matter was on display. As ridiculous as that would look on me, Dreya gives it a fiyah-type element. It's a good thing too, because it doesn't sound like Ms. Layla is trying to fool with Dreya.

"You look good," I say.

Dreya looks over from the mirror and says, "You too. That's a good look for you."

"Thanks."

"So," Dreya asks with her head cocked to one side, "you're going to prom with Dilly? How'd that end up going down?"

I shrug. "He's cool, and I didn't have a date, so it was a wrap sort of. I thought I didn't even care about going, but then I changed my mind."

"Your mom is gonna be cool with him going? With Carlos and everything?"

"We'll leave from the studio, right?"

Dreya laughs out loud and shakes her head. "Okay, even if we do leave from the studio, don't you think she's going to want to come and take pictures? We're talking about Auntie Shawn, queen of the digital camera."

"You're right. I just won't tell her about Dilly being related to Bryce and LaKeisha."

"You better hope she doesn't find out."

Dreya throws open the door to the back room like she's walking onto a stage. She struts out as if she's on a runway, and even strikes a little pose a few feet from Ms. Layla. I don't make nearly as bold of an entrance, but I give the cameras a little twirl. I can't be looking all boring next to the diva Drama.

Bethany woot-woots. "That's my girl! You are on fiyah!"

Notice that she says nothing about my hook up, and I wasn't the one who treated her like some old busted up groupie chick. But you know what? I don't care about her lodging herself inside of the crack of Dreya's butt, just like that bodysuit was all up in mine.

Mystique claps her hands, runs over to me, and hugs me tightly. "I like this outfit. Now, I just need to teach you how to dance."

I swallow a frown. I do not wish to share with the BET viewers the lack of dance skill in the Tolliver family blood. I mean, we've got mad singing talent. We can't have it all! Look at Ciara! She's singing about *riding* the beat, because she can dance her butt off. Who heard her singing about singing on a beat? Yeah, I didn't think so.

"I didn't think I needed dance lessons," I say through clenched teeth.

Mystique laughs out loud. "You're a lot better than Drama, but you still need some work. What do you think, Drama? You ready to learn some choreography for the tour?"

"I don't do choreography," Dreya announces. "I pop, that's about it."

Mystique scrunches her face with confusion. "You pop? What does that even mean?"

Dreya bends her knees and pops her booty over to one side, then rolls it back and pops it over to the other side. Then she drops into a squatting position and pops it in the middle. Bethany joins her. They look like two strippers up in here. I'm telling you, Dreya would snap that behind right off her hips if it wasn't attached. That's how hard she's popping.

"That's not dancing," Mystique says. "You can't really think that's going to be entertaining for a five song set."

"Pretty much," Dreya replies.

"Well, Big D wants me to teach you some moves for your video shoot for 'Love Is.' "

Dreya frowns. "Why is Big D asking you to do stuff for my video shoot and not asking me?"

Mystique doesn't answer, she only sighs, rolls her eyes, and shakes her head. Her body language tells me and everybody else that she's tired of Dreya. But the look is only momentary. The smile quickly reappears on Mystique's face.

"Choreography class for both of you. Tomorrow afternoon at two o'clock."

"But tomorrow is Sunday," Dreya whines.

"Have you got junior usher board committee meeting at church or something?" Mystique asks with a chuckle. "It'll be fun. We can do it over at Zac's house."

"Over at Zac's house? Why does it have to be over there?" Dreya asks. "I'd rather come to the studio."

"Because Zac had a dance studio built for me in the basement," Mystique explains. "All wood floors. Benji will be by to pick you up at 8:00 a.m. sharp. Eat a light breakfast, full of carbs. Y'all have a lot of work to do."

"We're going to celebrate my single's release tonight! I can't be getting up that early," Dreya moans.

Mystique promptly ignores her. Dreya opens her mouth to blurt out yet another protest, but is interrupted by a car horn blaring outside.

"Who is that outside my boutique honking like a maniac?" Ms. Layla fusses.

We all turn our attention to the storefront window. The car is a platinum drop-top Benz with a big pink bow on it. Truth walks around the car and leans against the passenger side with a huge grin on his face.

Dreya shrieks at the top of her lungs. "My man bought me a car!"

Dreya runs outside, and we all, including the cameraman, follow her. She hugs Truth around his neck and runs her fingers through his locs before she runs to the driver's side of the car and jumps in.

This ride is fly as all get out. It's got all the features too. Wood grain, smoky grey leather interior, chrome wheels accented with rhinestones, and tires glistening with Armor All. He even got her personalized plates that say MZ. DRAMA.

While everyone else is smiling and congratulating Dreya, I watch Bethany narrow her eyes and give Dreya one of the most haterrific glares I've ever seen. That look is more than a little bit of envy. Shoot, I'm envious! Being a pedestrian is for the birds. But that vibe that Bethany is giving out is pure hatred. It's one of those looks that you give a person when you don't think they're looking. But somebody is looking at Bethany. Me for one, but more important, the BET cameraman just caught her look and immortalized it on film.

She better hope that snippet ends up on the editing room floor.

7

Aunt Charlie blasts the radio from our living room. I think it's ghetto as what to turn the radio all the way up as high as it can go. But I guess it is Saturday night. It ain't like anybody has to go to school or work tomorrow.

But I know why she's doing it. Tonight on Hot 107.9, they're debuting Dreya's first single—"Love Is." I'm excited too, I ain't even gon' lie. Dreya's not even here to celebrate with us, though. Truth got her a suite at the downtown Omni at CNN Center so they could celebrate together.

He's such a good boyfriend. Not. The BET cameras are with them. And they even let Bethany tag along. I passed. I'd rather enjoy hearing my creation on the radio in the quiet privacy of my own home.

"This is it! Here go my baby!" Aunt Charlie squeals.

My mom shouts, "Turn it up!"

"It's all the way up," I mumble as if they can hear me over the roar of the DJ.

At least it's private, even if it's not quiet.

Manny comes out of his mother's bedroom, dragging behind him his favorite *Transformers* blanket.

"What's all this noise?" he asks, sounding like an eighty-year-old man.

"Boy, take your little behind back to bed," my mother says, "before you wind up getting a whipping."

"Why you gotta play me like that, Auntie Shawn? I was just trying to catch some zzz's, and y'all up here playing all this music."

Yes. He's five. I'ma need them to get his little ghetto superstar behind tested for Mensa or something. It don't even make sense for him to be that smart. Especially when he still pees in the bed.

Manny crawls up on the couch next to me. "What's poppin', cousin?"

"What's poppin' with you?" I ask.

"I asked you first," Manny says with a pout. "Did you or my sister blow up yet? I'm ready to move into a house with my own room. Y'all gonna make that happen anytime soon?"

"I hope so, little man. I want to move too! What kind of house do you want?" I ask.

"I want a mansion with ten bedrooms and a whole lotta bathrooms. That way when I wait til the last minute to go to the bathroom, there will be one close by."

"That's what's up, little man."

"Oh, and I want a whole *Transformers* room! Bed, pillows, curtains, sheets! I want Optimus Prime all up in that piece."

I burst out laughing. "Manny, you are too much."

"Yeah, he is," Aunt Charlie says. "And he better simmer down, before I send his little mannish self to bed."

"What's good, ATL?" blares from the radio. "Tonight we've got a debut from one of our own ripe Georgia peaches. Her name is Ms. Drama, and the song is called 'Love Is.' Hit me up on Twitter, and tell me if you love it or hate it."

I hear the first thirty-two bars of my composition light up the airwaves, and I feel a rush go through my body! This is hella exciting, even if Dreya's voice is caressing my lyrics.

It's a totally different feeling than when I did the hook on Truth's single. That was a tiny snippet in a song that someone else dreamed up. This is mine! Well, I guess Sam and I both wrote the lyrics, but the melody is mine.

Right after the bridge, there's a breakdown that's different than what I originally wrote. I scoot forward to the end of the couch and tilt my head toward the radio. Who had the audacity to mess with my music?

Then, I hear Truth's gravelly voice wind over the track. "Her love is fiyah, I'm a pocketful of matches / Strike up on her friction, leave the spot full of ashes / Take my blank check, but she don't even have to cash it / She strike a pose e'ry time she see them flashes."

See, now this is a hot mess right here. Who ever heard of putting some wack rhyme on the perfect mid-tempo ballad? Some songs don't need that hip-hop piece. And then Dreya's doing some ridiculous sounding runs too, like I haven't taught her any better.

But I bet people are gonna eat this up, so I'm gonna keep my anger bottled up on the inside. Don't want to get labeled as a hater!

My phone rings, and I have to get up and walk back to my bedroom to answer it. My mother and Aunt Charlie are still booty bumping and high-fiving to this song.

"Hello," I say when I close my bedroom door.

"What was *that?*" Sam asks. He sounds as irritated as I feel.

"That's the same thing I was sitting over here thinking. The song did not need any of that extra mess."

I hear Sam's annoyed exhale over the phone. "They took a piece of music and turned it into a wack, mediocre radio track. Hearing Truth's voice on there is freaking me the heck out."

"I wish they had asked my opinion," I complain. "But I guess that's just Big D flexin' and letting us know who's running Big D in the A Records."

"Yeah, well, he ain't running nothing over at Epsilon Records."

I laugh out loud. "What's that got to do with anything? We don't deal directly with Epsilon anyway. You're going through Big D, and I'm going through Mystique."

"Not for long, baby girl. I'm going to make a bid for an in-house songwriter gig with Epsilon. Maybe go up to New York a while after the tour. I've got to get out from under Big D's shadow."

"But won't that hurt Big D? He's gonna trip out if you leave him."

"The only thing that a person can be certain of in life is change. He's just gonna have to roll with it."

I chuckle. "You getting all lyrical and poetic, sounding the way a true songwriter is supposed to sound."

"Yeah, I guess."

Uncomfortable silence ensues. I hate uncomfortable silences.

I clear my throat and say, "So . . ."

"Why are you going to prom with Dilly?" Sam interrupts. "That's like a serious insult, you know. He's lamer than a mug."

"Your opinion. And I know you don't think that Rielle chick is a step up from me. I don't even think so."

"Okay, whatever. But I thought you didn't like him because he's Bryce's little brother. What happened to all that noise you were doing over at Zac's house? All that blowing up you were about to do?"

"I didn't say I was marrying the boy. I'm going to prom with him. . . ."

"And doing a song with him."

"That's business," I reply. "That has nothing to do with him being my prom date."

"Just be careful, Sunday. Bryce is real shady."

Hello? Earth to Sam. I already know that. I could probably prove that Bryce is shady to a jury of his peers, and I haven't taken one law class yet.

But since I want this conversation to end, I reply, "All right, Sam. I'll be careful."

Sam is tripping anyway. He doesn't get to care about who I go to prom with. He doesn't get to worry about who I'm crushing on. The only thing he gets to worry about, as far as I'm concerned, is this here music. And our single just played on the radio, so ain't nothing to worry about there. Know what I mean?

8

Eight o'clock in the morning is too early to be getting up and going over anybody's house. Especially when that person thinks you're about to do some kind of dance routine. This is what I call unnecessary roughness. Violation awarded to Mystique.

"Y'all can go ahead and stretch. Get loosened up. Hit those hamstrings, quads, glutes, and do some back stretches too. I'm going to get some Gatorade."

Mystique bounces out of her custom dance studio and up the stairs. The room reminds me of the ballet classes that Dreya and I were forced to take when we were seven. There's a bar attached to the wall that's a full mirror. The floors are shining like they've got ten coats of wax on them.

"Why do we need to do all those stretches?" Dreya asks. "She's making it sound like we're about to do some kind of workout video."

"I want to know why I even have to be here. It's your single! I'm not even done with my record yet. I should be at home working on music."

"Or with Sam at the lab," she says with a snicker.

"Why you say it like that?"

Dreya shrugs. "Because that's messed up that y'all still have to work with each other. I heard how he played you about prom."

Okay, Dreya is taking this forget-the-cameraman-is-there thing a little too seriously. We are not about to rehash my personal drama on TV.

"He didn't play me. I uninvited him. It's all good."

"Well, I knew y'all wasn't gonna make it after the fight with him and Truth. I mean he felt like you were pushing up on another dude."

I put both hands on my hips. "You and I both know I wasn't pushing up on Truth."

If anything Truth was pushing up on me. That night at the club and just about every day prior to that.

"Truth told me you weren't."

"So why are we talking about it?"

"I'm just saying why Sam is not checking for you. But Dilly is. He's cute, but . . . you know."

I widen my eyes at Dreya. We signed release forms that say they can basically put anything we say on national TV. She's tripping bringing up Dilly and *that* situation. Bryce and his shooting spree are definitely not ready for prime time family viewing. And then what about when my mom sees this? She would have a cow.

"Yes, I know. Think about my mom, Dreya. I don't

want to upset her, you know? She's already going through enough."

Mystique reappears with the drinks in hand. She sits them in a corner of the room.

"Are y'all warmed up?" she asks.

"Um, yeah, about that. We were just chitchatting because we don't know how to do all that stuff you said," Dreya says.

Mystique frowns. "Y'all don't know how to stretch? Y'all don't play sports?"

"We play music," I say.

Mystique does a few neck circles and stretches her arms over her head. "Okay, then let's start with the stretches."

She walks us through hamstring and calf stretches. Then, we stretch our backs and arms with a series of yoga-like moves. Then we do some deep breathing in a seated position on the floor.

I'm already tired, and we haven't started dancing yet.

"Now that y'all are warmed up, let's get to some real work."

Mystique walks over to the sound system that's built into the wall and presses a button. A fast, club track starts playing. Dreya and I look at each other, and I can tell my cousin and I for one rare instant are on the same page.

Mystique smiles at us. "I know this is fast, and it sounds nothing like your track, but we're gonna get our blood pumping on this one. Just follow me, like we're in an aerobics class."

Mystique starts with a one-two step that's pretty simple, but once me and Dreya get the hang of it, she adds a slide to the step. That's where she loses Dreya. I try to keep up, but after a slide to both sides, I'm hopelessly off beat.

"Drama, keep going," Mystique says. "If you're on stage and you mess up the choreography, you can't just stand there. Get used to recovering from a mistake."

Dreya rolls her eyes, and tries to start again. I know she's only being this dedicated because those cameras are rolling. She would've been gone if not for that.

I'm huffing and puffing like I weigh a thousand pounds, but it seems like Mystique is just getting started. She dips down to the floor in a half squat and then pops her body precisely to the beat. This is one of Dreya's favorite moves so she does it too.

"Your lower body has the right motion, but your upper body is stiff as a board," Mystique critiques. "Pop your shoulder blades back as you pop your hips. Switch your head from side to side. Make sure your whole body is either in motion or in preparation for motion."

Now Dreya does stop. "You think this is *Dancing with the Stars* or something? We can't do all that."

"Not today you can't," Mystique says, "but in a few weeks, by the time we go on tour, you'll be a lot hotter than you are right now."

For some reason, that bit of encouragement from Mystique gets me pumped. I close my eyes and try to catch the beat. I feel myself swaying from side to side, and then I start the one-two step again. Then the slides come naturally.

I open my eyes when the track ends, and Mystique is

beaming at me. "Sunday, that was hot. In a little bit, you'll be out-dancing me."

Dreya gives three hard claps. "Yeah, Sunday. You're a real natural."

There's a smile on Dreya's face, but the look in her eyes is pure hateration. I don't think Mystique notices, because she goes back to the sound system and changes the music. The intro to "Love Is" blares out of the speakers.

"Okay, Drama. I've been thinking of something really simple and hot for your video. We're going to have about twenty female dancers, and you'll be at the front. They'll fan out behind you like a pyramid."

Mystique starts dancing, doing very fluid motions. On some parts it even looks like she's moving in slow motion. I can imagine how hot this would look with twenty girls doing it.

"It's supposed to look like synchronized swimming," Mystique explains. "Except that you're standing up."

Dreya flares her nose as if the dance has a horrible odor. She folds her arms across her chest to emphasize her displeasure with the dance.

Mystique turns the music off. "You don't like it?"

"No. I think it's obvious that I don't," Dreya says.

Mystique stretches her arms over her head. "I spent a lot of time on that choreography, Drama. The least you could do is try it out."

"No. The least I can do is *not* try it."

Dreya snatches up her stuff. "That's why I drove myself, I knew she was going to try to hold us prisoner. Sunday, if you're riding with me, come on."

"I want to learn some more. I'll catch a ride home with Benji."

Dreya sneers in my direction. "You're really playing that protégée role, huh. It fits you."

"What role are you playing?" Mystique asks. "You keep that diva thing up, it's gonna be unemployed R & B chick."

Dreya looks over at the cameras and glares at Mystique. Then, she spins on one heel and storms out of the studio.

I'm lightweight tripping myself that Mystique played Dreya like that with the cameras rolling. Yeah, she needs a reality check, but dang. This is TV. You can't take that back.

"Don't worry. That won't end up on the show. I'll make sure of it," Mystique assures me as if she's reading my mind.

I really hope Mystique is telling the truth about this, because no matter what, Dreya is my cousin. I've got to have her back even when I don't want to, because that's how Tollivers roll.

9

"Honey, you look gorgeous!"

I beam a huge smile at my mother, as I do a little spin in the studio lounge. I'm wearing my fitted, money green, sequin-covered dress. Mystique's personal hair-stylists and makeup artists are here with us at the studio helping us get ready for prom. And of course, the BET film crew is recording it all.

Aunt Charlie struts around the studio lounge flipping her platinum blond lace front that she bought specifically for this occasion. I'm not even going to talk about the platinum mink eyelashes that she's rocking. Wait. Yes, I am. She looks like Lambchop from the 'hood.

Aunt Charlie slaps Big D a high five. "My baby is on fiyah, ain't she?"

I'm so tired of people saying *on fiyah* this and *on fiyah* that. Not too long ago, I remember people said somebody was burning and that wasn't a good thing. Now it's the hotter the better.

Big D laughs at Aunt Charlie doing the Stanky Leg dance. "Yes, Ms. Tolliver. She is on fiyah."

Aunt Charlie immediately stops dancing and frowns. "Ms. Tolliver was my mama! Or maybe my big Sister Shawn. I'm Charlie, baby."

Manny, who's standing right next to Aunt Charlie, gives his mother a wide-eyed, glazed-over stare. Then, he looks dead into the camera before tugging Aunt Charlie's leg.

"What you need, baby boy?" she asks.

"Um, can you find me some juice, *Charlie?*"

Everybody bursts into laughter as Aunt Charlie's face scrunches into a frown. She lunges toward Manny as he tries to escape a smack on the butt.

Chuckling, my mother asks, "When are the boys getting here?"

My heart rate speeds up just a little. Everyone knows not to say anything about Dilly being related to Bryce. We even gave Mystique a little bit of a cover story. We told her that my mom went to school with LaKeisha and they had beef back then. We couldn't tell her the whole story, but we needed to let her know enough so that she'd help keep my mom in the dark.

Big D responds to my mother, "Soon, Ms. Tolliver. Sam went to scoop Dilly and Truth. I don't know how Bethany's date is getting here, but he better come on with the come on. When the limo gets here it's a wrap."

I force a smile onto my face to keep from frowning.

Bethany is going with my ex-boyfriend Romell. I don't want him as a part of my prom night or on our TV show.

My mother asks, "Who is Dilly again? I don't think you've introduced us. I thought you were going with Sam."

"Mom, I told you about Sam. Dilly is an Epsilon artist, and he's nice. You'll like him, I promise."

She pokes out her lips. "I guess. But I don't think I'll like him more than I like Sam."

"They need to hurry up," Dreya says. "I said I wanted to be fashionably late, but dang!"

Dreya fluffs up her little spiky hairdo, and runs a hand over her platinum gown. I was surprised that she wanted to wear a floor length dress. It's very classy, and very anti-Dreya. Her accessories are silver and rhinestone. She's got big rhinestone earrings, and she's also got them on her shoes. My favorite piece of her ensemble is her silver Egyptian bracelet that winds up her arm like a metal snake.

Bethany's look, in my opinion, reminds me of one of those girls from the *Flavor of Love* show. Her dress is a red spandex halter, and she's got bare legs and clear platform shoes. The result is the opposite of fly. But then again we are talking about Bethany.

Aunt Charlie and Manny come back into the lounge, her sashaying like she's on a runway and him sipping his favorite thing in the world—somebody else's juice.

"Girl, you are bad to the bone," Aunt Charlie says to Dreya. "Ain't my baby bad to the bone?"

I believe we've already given Dreya enough compliments on her badness! Aunt Charlie pops her fingers and dances to a song that only she can hear. She really needs to sit herself down somewhere before she pulls a muscle or something. I laugh quietly inside when the cameraman shoots in the opposite direction of Aunt Charlie.

Finally, the guys are here. Truth is wearing a standard white tux, but his platinum tuxedo shirt is anything but the norm. He does a little twirl for the camera, then he pulls Dreya into his arms and gives her a big bear hug. And Sam is here, too! Why, why, why!

"Sam," I say, "you came!"

"I did," he says with a grin.

"Dude . . . really? Why did you come?"

"I want to see my friends off to prom! Truth and Big D came over when I left."

"They came to see you and Rielle off to prom?"

"Yeah . . . you had to bring that up, Sunday?"

"You're the one who brought up your prom."

"Boy! You better not mess up my hair!" Dreya fusses.

"All three of y'all look good, but y'all ain't got nothing on my baby!" Truth declares as he takes in me and Bethany.

Bethany rolls her eyes and goes to open the door for Romell who just pulled up outside. I swallow hard and try to avoid Sam's gaze. It doesn't seem right for him to be standing here in an Aeropostale tee and jeans instead of a tuxedo.

Dilly's money green vest matches my dress perfectly. He smells great too. But I'm tripping wishing that Sam was my date and not Dilly.

Sam kisses my mom on the cheek. "Hey, Ms. Tolliver."

"Hey, Sam. Did you bring me one of your prom pictures? It was last night, right?"

I look away and swallow again. Why'd she have to bring up his prom?

Dilly takes me by the hand and spins me around. "You look great, Sunday!"

I could hug him for changing the subject. I try to make my face look as happy as I possibly can. "You do too, Dilly-Dill. You look like a million bucks."

He laughs. "I wish I had a million bucks, I do in my head / But I'd take a million of your kisses instead."

"The freestyle king!" Big D says with a laugh. "You always got a rhyme ready don't you?"

Dilly shrugs and smiles at me. "Only when I'm inspired."

Now, I'm blushing. Dilly's getting under my skin, even though I don't want him there. I think he's getting under Sam's skin too, but not in a good way. Sam abruptly leaves the room, and I can't think of a thing to say to make him stay, nor do I want to. I'm getting high from all this attention from Dilly.

"Romell is up in the spot!"

Why did this fool bust up in the room dancing like he's on *Stomp the Yard* or something? He looks so stupid right now. And Bethany looks like she can't figure out if she should be embarrassed.

She should be.

Dreya rolls her eyes at him. She never did like Romell, not even when he and I were kicking it. "Come on, let's go. The limo is outside."

"Wait," Romell says. "Big D, can I do an impromptu audition for you?"

Big D's eyebrows scrunch into a frown. "Right now, man? Y'all 'bout to go to prom."

"It won't take long. I've been working on some stuff for you."

I guess Romell isn't done hamming it up for the BET video crew. Truth rolls his eyes, and Dilly pulls me toward the door. Poor Bethany (I actually do feel sorry for her) looks like she wants to hide in a corner.

Romell starts bobbing his head to an imaginary beat. "I rocks the proper way / Stuntin' in the A / All day e'ry day / What can I say?"

Oh, my goodness. He couldn't be any worse. I was hoping that he had at least a little bit of skill. It's a good thing we're seniors, because he'd never last another school year at Decatur High after this airs on BET. They'd laugh him right up out of the school.

Manny says, "Dude, that was lame!"

Dreya and Truth burst into laughter, and I struggle very hard not to join them.

Big D says, "I'll let you know when Big D in the A Records is auditioning for new talent. Keep practicing, dawg." Surprisingly he keeps a straight face as he says this.

Bethany grabs Romell by the arm and pulls him out of the studio. And since it's time to go we follow closely behind.

As I walk past him, Sam touches my shoulder. "Have fun, Sunday."

I shudder as I look down at his hand on my bare skin.

Why does he have to be here? Why is he standing here with his arm around my mother and touching my shoulder? Now, I just know that I'm not going to enjoy my prom—at all. I'm going to spend the entire evening thinking of this moment.

"Thanks, Sam," I say and turn to go.

Dilly puts his arm around me as we walk to the limo. "It's okay, Sunday. I know I'm not the one you want to share this evening with, but I hope you have a really good time anyway."

I stop in my tracks. Dilly is so mature for a junior in high school.

"Don't feel like that. I'm happy to be going with you," I reply.

He lifts his eyebrows and grins, "Yeah?"

"Yep. Let's go and turn this prom out!"

Dilly gives me a strange look, like he doesn't believe what I'm saying. I mean, it's not like he was my first choice by any stretch of the imagination, but that doesn't mean he's a bad choice. He's cooler than cool, sweeter than sweet, and finer than fine.

That might have sounded lamer than lame, but I'm doing me right now. Know what I mean?

Okay, wow! Our prom should be called groupie central! Not only is everybody riding hard on Dreya and Truth, but they are hamming it up like crazy for the BET camera crew. Girls dancing all hard and popping their booties like it's a casting call for the next Ludacris video, and dudes spitting random wack rhymes.

I'm embarrassed to be a student at Decatur High.

Dreya, on the other hand, is eating this up. She and Truth are in the center of a crowd like they're the king and queen of the world and not just our prom. I fade to the side of the room with Dilly so that I can have a moment's rest from the cameras.

"They really diggin' Drama, huh?" Dilly asks. "Must be that single playing on the radio."

"Pretty much. It doesn't take much for this crew here," I say.

Dilly laughs out loud. "Some people are just natural born groupies."

"Yeah, I guess."

He pulls a chair out from an empty table, and I take a seat. He sits down next to me. "Your girl Bethany seems like she likes the attention too."

"Man, I think she likes it more than Dreya."

"So what about you, Sunday? You don't crave the spotlight?" Dilly asks.

"I like it, but I definitely don't crave it."

He laughs again. "At least you know what you want."

"Right."

The principal of our school, Ms. Washburn, takes the microphone on the stage and signals to the DJ to stop the music.

"Hey there, Decatur High seniors!" she calls out.

The senior class roars, claps, and stomps in response. They so 'hood!

"We've got a special treat for the Decatur High class of 2010! Epsilon Records recording artists Truth, Drama, and Sunday Tolliver are going to perform tonight at your prom!"

I stand up in my seat and nearly knock my chair over. We're going to do what, when, and for whom? Stop the dang presses. Didn't nobody ask me about singing at my prom. This ain't a concert!

Before I can raise too many objections, Dreya and Truth are on the stage, and the track to "Love Is" is blasting from the speakers. They seem so comfortable with all this that I have to wonder if they knew about it in advance, and if they did, what exactly would be the point of *not* telling me.

Of course, they get the crowd pumped, because that's what they do. Dreya whips around her long dress as she sings, just like she practiced this whole thing, and Truth moves back and forth across the stage as if he had one or two rehearsals as well.

Something stinks to high heaven up in this piece.

When they're done, everyone turns to look at me. And of course they do. They're ready for the rest of the concert.

"You going up there?" Dilly asks.

"It doesn't look like I have much of a choice."

The crowd parts down the middle as I walk up to the stage, all eyes on me. I'm not nervous, because I've performed before. But I am wondering what people will think of my song. It's nothing like Dreya's, even though I wrote hers too.

Finally, I'm on stage and standing in front of the microphone. I look down and close my eyes until I hear the track start.

I hear the introductory bars of my masterpiece, and

forget where I am and who's staring at me. I just sway to the music, lean my head back, and open up my mouth.

By the time I get to the hook, I fade out of my trance and can hear my classmates clapping along with the beat.

By the second time I sing the hook, they're singing along with me. "Can you see me? Can you see me? Tell me what you want me to do, 'cause I wanna see me with you."

When I finish the song, I give the Decatur High class of 2010 a tiny head nod. For a moment, there's silence, but then they burst into applause.

And I don't know if the BET cameras can tell the difference, but I'm pretty sure they're cheering louder for me than they did for Dreya.

10

"So, how do you feel about going on tour with Truth and Sam after they got into the fight at the club?"

I'm in my first confessional with a BET producer named Chad. I can't call him by name, or even act like I'm answering his question. These confessionals are supposed to sound like me giving random thoughts. And for real, why would I be willingly or randomly talking about that fight on BET?

"I feel cool about going on tour with Truth and Sam."

I carefully choose my words. I know what happens on these reality shows. As soon as you say something halfway crazy, it ends up on the show. They'll never catch me slipping.

"But what about their beef? Don't you think that might be kind of uncomfortable?"

"There is no beef."

"So are you and Sam back talking? He didn't go to your prom, but are y'all together again?"

"Sam and I are really great friends.

The interviewer looks frustrated that I'm not giving him anything to work with. "So what about your cousin? Are you friends with her?"

I swallow and pause before answering. "We're first cousins. She's the closest thing I have to a sister."

"You didn't answer my question."

"Your question was stupid."

Now Chad is frowning at me. I don't care. He'll have to edit that part out, I suppose.

"How do you feel about missing graduation?"

My eyes widen. "Excuse me? Missing graduation?"

"What? Big D didn't tell you? They changed the first tour stop, and it falls on your graduation day."

I stand up from the hard wooden stool they've got me sitting on and bust up out of the makeshift confessional booth.

"Sunday, we're not finished," Chad says.

"Later."

I rip through the studio looking for Big D, and I find him in the lounge chilling on the leather couch with Shelly. They're eating microwave popcorn, sipping on Coke, and watching a movie. Neither one of them look like they're in the mood to deal with my tirade, but oh well. Big D should've told somebody something.

I stand directly in their line of sight to the TV and fuss. "You scheduled a concert on my graduation day, Big D?"

For a second Big D looks confused. "No, baby girl.

You know that's not how that went down. I didn't change it. Epsilon Records found a new venue for y'all in Birmingham, so they moved the start date up."

"When were you planning on telling me?" I ask.

"It just slipped my mind, I guess. I meant to tell you. It's no biggie."

I shake my head and feel my body tremble with rage. "What do you mean it's no biggie? It's my graduation! I'm my mother's only daughter, Big D! I'm the only kid she's gonna get to see walk across that stage with a cap and gown on. How could you?"

Big D looks irritated, but doesn't move from his position on the couch. Shelly rolls her eyes like I'm wrecking her flow or something. Whatever! This is not a diva routine; I'm in trip out mode for real!

"It's not like you're not still getting your diploma," Big D reasons. "Your mama gets to see you on stage singing for the world to see. You think she's gonna care about some dry graduation ceremony?"

I cross my arms over my chest and nod. "I think she's gonna care, just like I care."

Big D clears his throat, hands Shelly the popcorn, and leans forward on the couch. He gives me that exasperated look that he usually saves for Dreya when she's tripping on something. Well, maybe it's time for someone else besides her to bring the drama.

"Baby girl, you've got a great opportunity right here that you're trying to mess up. You can't have it all, you know. Sometimes you gotta give to get."

I feel hot tears stinging my eyes. I know what it means when Big D starts reasoning with me like this and calling me "baby girl." It means that ain't nothing gonna change, so I might as well suck it up.

"At least you got to go to prom," Shelly says. "I was at a photo shoot on my prom night."

My eyes dart over at her. "Do you regret missing it?"

She shrugs. "Maybe I did for a minute, but after a while I really didn't care about it."

"See," Big D says, "You'll forget all about this when you blow up. Matter of fact, we'll have a graduation party while you're on the road. How 'bout that?"

How can I explain to Big D that while his offer is thoughtful, it's not enough?

When I don't reply, Big D continues, "You could always *not* go with us to Birmingham. You could meet us in the next city. It's going to cost Epsilon Records money, and they're not going to like it at all. It's your decision."

"My decision?" I ask in a tiny, tiny voice.

Big D shrugs and leans back into the couch cushions. "Yeah, so you do what you feel you gotta do. Now, can me and Shelly please finish watching this movie?"

I move out of their way and head back downstairs to finish my confessional. I'm on the verge of tears now, but I'm sure that Chad will parlay that into some drama-filled TV moment. It's whatever.

Once I'm back sitting on the stool, Chad asks, "So, where were we? Graduation. How do you feel about missing it?"

"I don't know how I feel about missing graduation, Chad. I don't know if I'm going to miss it."

Chad's eyes light up as if I've given him something juicy to work with. I guess this will make for good reality

TV. Too bad it's my life we're talking about here, and not a desperate housewife.

I know I've got to make a decision—and soon. Missing my graduation was nowhere on my agenda, but missing out on the tour and maybe even my music career? That's not where I want to be either.

Why do I wish I had a friend right about now? Where my peeps at? It sure is lonely at the top.

I stumble out of the confessional booth, and Sam is standing right there, like he's waiting on me. He's got a really sympathetic look on his face, like he already knows what's up. When he holds his arms out to me for a hug, I burst into tears.

I melt into his embrace and listen to his soothing whispers in my ear. "You know graduation isn't really all that important, right? I'll skip mine if you have to skip yours."

"You don't have to do that," I say as I look up into his face. "It's bad enough I have to miss my own."

"It's called solidarity. Something friends do for each other."

I couldn't wipe the smile off my face if I tried. I do have some peeps after all.

Sam continues, "You never did give me one of your prom pictures."

"You want a picture of me and Dilly at prom?" I ask.

"I want a picture of you in that green dress."

11

I'm having a marathon recording session at Zac's house with Mystique, Sam, and Dilly. The plan is to get at least half of my songs completed before we go on our six-week tour. Then I'll record the rest right before I start my freshman year of college.

Sounds like a lot, doesn't it?

Sam and I have already worked on some melodies and hooks and created tracks to fit them. Mystique wrote me a song, too. It's all right, not exactly what I'd call a hit, but I knew she'd leave her mark on my album. Now, it's all on me to come up with the rest of the lyrics, and that's easier said than done.

"You need water or something, Sunday?" Dilly asks.

Since I'm working on a ballad today, we don't even need him here, but I'm glad that he is. Any friendly face is welcome when I've got to deal with Mystique cracking the whip.

"Sing me the hook again," Mystique says. She's in all work mode now. Totally serious, hair weave tied back in a scarf, no makeup on.

I swallow, take a deep breath, and let loose, "You've got a need / to just believe / so just believe in you / A dream deferred can still come true / A dream deferred can still come true."

"I like the way you sound on the hook. You sound so inspirational, like an old Whitney Houston song."

"Thanks," I reply, "but I'm having a problem with the verses. Everything I come up with sounds corny."

"Let me take a stab at it," Mystique says. "Play the track, Sam."

Mystique closes her eyes as the music fills the room. Sam has created a lush, melodic piano track, and like me, Mystique can't stand still while she listens to it. She rocks back and forth while her head bobs in time with the slow beat.

She sings, "Have you ever had your dream deferred and your life stays the same? / Have you ever woken up to find that nothing seems to change? / Did you just give up, just give in? / Think that you can't win? / Or did you realize that tomorrow, your destiny can begin?"

Sam chimes in, "Just hold on / Don't stop now / 'Cause just around the corner there is a chance for you . . ."

I come back with the hook again, "You've got a need / to just believe / so just believe in you / A dream deferred can still come true. / A dream deferred can still come true."

Mystique claps her hands and jumps up and down. "I love it! Dilly, why don't you help us on the second verse?"

Dilly? Does he sing too? Nobody mentioned that to me!

He clears his throat and closes his eyes, causing those gorgeous eyelashes to brush his cheeks. "I know it seems like tomorrow / might not ever come. / But a champion might lose some games / before ever winning one."

I jump back in, "Keep pressing on / keep going strong / Victory is in sight. / You can only know what the end will be / if you step out on faith and try."

Sam sings the bridge again, and then we all sing the hook. Mystique's contralto, my soprano, Dilly's alto, and Sam's tenor make a wonderful sound. The harmonies are easy and perfect—just like a miniature choir.

Mystique says, "We might want to clean up the lyrics a bit, but I think I like it for the most part. Dilly and Sam, I want y'all to sing backup on this track. I like the sound of male voices on here. It makes it sound more soulful."

When Dilly doesn't say anything, we all stop and stare. He's got a pained look on his face that seems so sorrowful that I reach out and touch his hand.

"You okay?" I ask.

He nods. "It's the words to this song. I mean, y'all are living out the dream, but mine, well, it's kind of on the back burner. I guess it hit home a little bit."

I swallow over the huge lump in my throat. He sounds so sad that it makes me want to cry!

"It's coming soon, Dilly," Mystique says. "You've just got to hold on a little bit."

"I know. I'm cool. It was just the song, and Sunday's voice I guess," he replies.

Sam's eyebrows knit together in a frown, but he doesn't

make a response. He taps a tune out on the keyboard, and looks at the floor.

Mystique's eyes light up, and her mouth forms a little 'o' as if she's just struck gold. "How about this, Dilly? Why don't you go on the summer tour with us? You'd be a roadie, of course, but since Sam is the assistant music director now, we kinda need an extra one."

"Are you serious?" Dilly asks, jumping to his feet.

"I am! You'll learn a lot, and I'm sure you'll end up on the reality show."

Sam stops tapping the keys and looks up at me. I shrug and give him a confused expression. What am I supposed to do about Mystique inviting someone on the tour? She's the princess of Epsilon Records, not me.

"Y'all cool with that?" Mystique asks. She looks from me to Sam as if she's trying to read our unspoken signals.

"I'm cool with it," Sam says. "But it's not like anybody cares about my opinion anyway."

"Everybody on this team matters," Mystique says. "And that's for real."

I bite my bottom lip, because I'm deep in thought. Dilly going on tour with us is all good, and it'll probably help move up his record release date, but what about Bryce and LaKeisha? Are they going to try to come too, and maybe even mug it up for the cameras on our reality show?

I know one thing. They haven't built a tour bus big enough for me to ride on with that drive-by shooting Bryce.

12

Dreya's eighteenth birthday is on this coming Wednesday, the day before we leave on our tour, and of course, she plans to have an all-out bash. She and Bethany have been planning for over a month, and I've caught a few snippets here and there, but pretty much everything has been top secret.

We just got a box in the mail addressed to Dreya. I'm thinking it's either a gift or something related to her party. Since she isn't here and Aunt Charlie is, my aunt feels it is her duty and right to open up mail addressed to her daughter.

My mother says, "Charlie, I don't think you should open that. What if it's one of Dreya's birthday presents? She wouldn't appreciate you opening that."

Aunt Charlie looks like she is considering my mother's warning. Then, she lifts the box up into the air and shakes it.

"This don't sound like no present," Aunt Charlie decides. "It sounds like cards or something."

"Isn't opening someone else's mail a federal offense?" I ask my mother. She should know, since she works at the post office carrying mail herself.

"Yes, it is, but since Dreya is her minor daughter, I don't think anyone would be able to press charges."

"That's right! So mind ya bidness, Sunday, and hand me a knife so I can cut this tape."

I slide Aunt Charlie a butter knife from the table and have a seat. As long as she's the one who's opening Dreya's mail, I want to see what it is too.

"What in the . . . ?" Aunt Charlie pulls a postcard out of the box.

Aunt Charlie's got such a crazy expression on her face that my mother and I both reach into the box and pull out a card too.

Immediately, I see why Aunt Charlie is looking crazy. The cards are invitations to Dreya's birthday celebration at Club Pyramids. She's standing on some kind of platform wearing a very skimpy bathing suit. Her hair and body look wet in the black-and-white photo, and the only streak of color is red lipstick.

Dreya looks like a video vixen in this photo. It's waaay too seductive for my taste, and apparently for Aunt Charlie's too, because she looks ready to explode.

"Oh my, she sure looks sexy," my mother says.

"She looks like a stripper," Aunt Charlie replies. "I'm breaking my foot off in somebody's behind."

"Whose behind? Dreya's? She's the one who took the

picture," I say. "You can't blame anyone else for this but her."

Aunt Charlie shakes her head and waves a stack of postcards in the air. "Nah, this here ain't my baby's doing. This was Truth and Big D. They trying to pimp my baby out."

"I doubt if Big D has anything to do with this," I say.

"What makes you think that?" Aunt Charlie grills. "It ain't like he's a saint or something."

"Oh, I didn't say that. But I know that Big D is real pressed about our tour sponsors. He would've nixed that with a quickness."

"Give me some scissors, Sunday," Aunt Charlie says.

"Why? What are you gonna do?" I ask.

"Just hand me the scissors!

I walk into the kitchen, reach into the utility drawer, and retrieve my mother's craft scissors. I walk back toward Aunt Charlie with my hand outstretched, but I'm almost afraid to hand them to her while she's looking so angry. Her face is wearing a scowl that makes her look like a pit bull.

When I continue to hesitate, Aunt Charlie snatches the scissors from my hand. She picks up about ten cards from the box and begins to cut them every which way. Then she grabs another stack and does the same thing. She looks down at the cut pieces on the table and stabs at the picture with the scissors.

"Hey!" shouts Dreya as she and Bethany walk through the front door. "Are those my invitations?"

Fortunately, Dreya got here before Aunt Charlie destroyed the whole box of postcards. Unfortunately, the BET crew is following her and getting all of the action on film.

"They *were* your invitations," Aunt Charlie replies. "You aren't handing out these filthy-looking things."

"Filthy? What do you mean filthy? This picture is fly as what!" Dreya pulls the box out of Aunt Charlie's grasp.

"Fo' sho'," Bethany says. "You look hawt on this postcard. All them chickens gonna envy you when they see it."

"Dreya, why would you want to have your body exposed like that?" my mother asks. "My sister raised you better than that."

Dreya rolls her eyes and sucks her teeth. "There you go, Auntie Shawn, being all dramatic. My mama mighta raised me some kind of way, but I'm 'bout to be grown. It's a whole lot of changes going down once I turn eighteen."

"What kind of changes?" Aunt Charlie asks.

Bethany clears her throat and looks away like she doesn't have anything to say. She sure was bumping her gums a few seconds ago, and now she's all speechless.

"Number one, I'm moving out. When our tour is over, my own crib is gonna be waiting for me. Number two, ain't nobody handling my money but me. I've already opened up bank accounts in my name only."

Aunt Charlie has this dumbfounded look on her face like Dreya just slapped her or something. I'm not surprised at all about this. Like who didn't know that she was moving out? She's probably moving in with Truth.

"You're moving in with that lowlife, aren't you?" my mother asks.

"If you're talking about my boyfriend, he is not a lowlife. He is a platinum recording artist," Dreya argues.

"I don't care how many records he sells, he's a lowlife to me."

Dreya puffs her cheeks out and then blows the air out of her mouth like a whistle. "For your information, I'm not moving in with Truth. Bethany's coming to stay with me so I won't be by myself."

Wow. Dreya and Bethany as roommates? Talk about keeping your enemies close.

"Are you moving out too, Sunday?" my mother asks. "Let me know now."

How did I get in this conversation? I'm an innocent bystander here!

"I'm not moving out, until I go to Spelman. I'm not spending my money on an apartment."

Dreya lifts her box under her arm and motions with her head toward the door. "Come on, Bethany, let's be out."

The BET film crew gets one last shot of Aunt Charlie as she sits down at the table still holding the scissors in her hand. Little bits of postcard are littered all around.

"She's getting her own place. . . ." Aunt Charlie says as Dreya shuts our front door. "I thought we would all move together. That Sunday and Dreya would get our whole family a house in Buckhead or something when the money started coming in. But she's leaving us here."

Dreya is on some other kind of foul stuff. Her mama

has been ride or die for her since before a record deal. I mean, Auntie Charlie would fight anybody for Dreya. She'd do the same for Manny, me, and my mom too.

Dreya said that a lot of things were gonna change when she turned eighteen, but I think the biggest change of all is that she's forgetting that she's a Tolliver. That's not a good look, at all.

13

Everybody should've known that Dreya was going to find a way to make her eighteenth birthday party unforgettable. Even if that means making it full of drama. As soon as Aunt Charlie and I step inside Club Pyramids, we already know what's up. My mom didn't come for the obvious reasons, but surprisingly she didn't get on me and Auntie Charlie for coming to Bryce's club.

We came late so the party is already going on. Dreya's music is booming from the speakers, and she's strutting around the place in a bustier, booty shorts, and lace pantyhose. Bethany is dressed exactly like her except with different colors. Can anyone say swagger jack?

I feel kind of underdressed in my khaki miniskirt, baby tee, and jean jacket. At least my hair is down, and I'm wearing heels. Aunt Charlie is doing the do, though! She is not about to be outdressed by the lame chicks! She's got on a platinum blond, mid-back length lace front wig, and a Deréon sundress. It would be messed up if she didn't look young in the face too. Aunt Charlie looks good for thirty-six years old! Young guys try to push up on her all the time.

"All right, Sunday, meet me by the door at midnight, if you're riding home with me," Aunt Charlie says. "I'm about to go over here and make sure none of these goons are running up on my daughter."

"Okay, Aunt Charlie."

I scan the jam-packed club, looking for someone to chill with. I see the BET camera crew and definitely know I want to steer clear of them. I'm in chill mode right now, and not trying to watch what I say because it might end up on TV.

Since I don't see anybody I know who's within shout-out range, I take a seat in the VIP area. It's pretty dead in here, because Dreya's out on the floor with her adoring fans. It's her party so everybody wants to be where she is. Except me!

The last person I want to see walks into the VIP section as soon as I sit down. Truth has his locs tied back, and he's got on a nice Sean John jean hookup. I'm against skinny jeans on boys, but Truth has the swagger to pull it off.

"This where you hiding? Why don't you come out here and join the party?" Truth asks.

"Naw. Go ahead." I reply. "I'ma just do me right here. Get me a soda and chill."

Truth laughs. "Why you come to a party and you don't want to participate?"

"So that no one can say I didn't come! I'd rather be at the house honestly."

Truth sits down in the booth across from me. I do not recall inviting him to sit down. This is how drama pops off.

"You ready for the tour?" he asks, like we're just buddies having a normal conversation.

"Yeah, Mystique and I have been practicing my show and what not. It's tight."

Truth smiles. "Mystique is one hundred percent about her business, so I know y'all get along."

"Yeah, we do. She and Dreya—not so much."

Truth shakes his head and sighs. I can barely hear him over the loud music, but his body language tells me he's frustrated.

"I keep telling Drama to listen to Mystique, but she ain't hearing it."

"That's *your* girlfriend. You need to let her know what's up."

"Or I could just stop dealing with her altogether."

Instinctively, I look from left to right to see if there's a camera crew anywhere. I don't see one, but I notice the small microphone taped at the top of Truth's shirt. He's tripping if he thinks I'm about to say something about my cousin while he's wearing a mic!

I play along, though, and don't let him know I see his microphone. "If you stop dealing with her that would be messed up. We're going on tour together, so if you plan on breaking up with her, I'd appreciate it if you'd do it after the tour."

Truth laughs. "Yeah, that would probably be the easiest thing for all of us."

Since Truth is determined to have a conversation with me, I ask, "Have you seen her new apartment yet?"

Truth sits back in the booth and makes himself comfortable—too comfortable if you ask me. He doesn't look like he plans on getting up anytime soon.

"Yeah, it's nice. It's got three bedrooms and two bathrooms. Drama's got her bedroom tricked all the way out with animal prints and leather. Bethany's room is tight too."

I chuckle. "How is it that she's getting the money to pay for all of this?"

"You know Epsilon and Big D got that on lock. Epsilon's been a little bit more generous since her single came out and got gold iTunes sales the first week."

I feel sick to my stomach. I sold Big D that song for one thousand dollars, and they've already sold five hundred thousand downloads. I can't help but feel played.

"So when does she get a check?" I ask.

"Why does she need a check when the bills are paid?" Truth asks.

I shake my head. He can't really be this stupid. I think he's playing with me, trying to get me to say something crazy into the microphone.

"She needs a check, so she can know exactly how much money she has and pay her own bills."

"Drama isn't like you, Sunday. She never has to see a check, as long as she's got money in her pocket."

That's one thing Truth and I agree on. Dreya is nothing like me.

"You better get back to the princess of this party before she comes looking for you and finds you over here in VIP chilling with me," I say.

"No doubt. You want me to tell Sam you're over here?"

I shake my head and smile. "He'll find me if he's looking for me."

Truth laughs out loud. "I see you, Sunday. Maybe you want me to tell Dilly to come over to VIP and hang with you."

"Hahaha. That's where you're wrong. I don't want anyone to be told to come and hang with me."

Truth gives me a fist bump and walks away from the table, and he can barely get across the room without people stopping him to say hi, congratulations, or whatever else. I do find it really strange that Bethany is waiting near the door to the VIP area. I watch her whisper something in Truth's ear, and then I watch him snatch off that little microphone that he thought I didn't see.

Then, Bethany pulls him out of the VIP area and off somewhere else, so I can't see the rest. Something is up with that, I just don't know what.

Instead of one of the boys finding me, Mystique pops up into the VIP area. It's a good thing she showed up, because I was just about to find myself a ride home from this party.

She and Benji slide into my booth. Benji's long, loose curls flow over his shoulder and across the T-shirt he's wearing. Mystique's wearing a tiny, black dress that is way too classy for this crowd.

"You look bored," Mystique notes. "Why are you sitting in here, when the party is going on out there?"

"I'm camera shy. Don't feel like being a TV star tonight."

Mystique pokes out her bright red, glossed lips. "I can get with that. But we're taping the countdown to the tour show! You don't want it to be all about Drama's birthday party, do you?"

I want to tell Mystique that I don't really care what it's about at this point. But I don't. Because she's sitting here looking at me, and something in her eyes reminds me that she gave me this opportunity so I better not mess it up.

"Come on," she says. "I'll go with you. You can make your entrance with me. That'll take some of the attention off of Drama."

I open my mouth to give a weak protest, but Mystique is already pulling me out of the booth and leading me to the door.

She appraises my look. "Cute outfit. I don't know if it's party material, but it's too late for me to pick something out for you."

I don't respond to Mystique's dissing of my outfit. Number one, I don't care, and number two, I know she's not trying to be mean.

Benji stays a half step behind us as we make our way over to the DJ booth. Finally, I see Sam. He's standing with Truth next to the door of the booth. He looks good in an all black tee, black jeans, and black boots. The only thing to break up all the dark color is a silver chain on his neck. He's even wearing his black rimmed glasses, looking like the nerd that he is.

Mystique swings open the door to the DJ booth and lets herself in. Nobody stops her. Maybe it's because she's a platinum-selling national recording artist. Or maybe it's because Benji's giving everyone evil, "I wish you would" glares.

I don't know whether I should go with Mystique into the booth or just stay outside with the crowd. I decide not to follow her, in case Dreya is in there or there's any other potential for mess popping off.

"Sunday," Sam calls from a few feet away where he and Truth are still standing. "Come here."

I don't know who he thinks he's talking to. Come here? Really? I'm so tired of people getting me confused.

When he sees that I'm ignoring him, he decides to walk himself over. That's his best be if he's trying to have a conversation with me. I wouldn't walk over to him now if I was starving to death and he had a bunch of Cinnabons hanging around his neck.

"Hey, Sunday. You lookin' good, ma."

"Thanks, Sam. You too."

"You want to dance?" he asks.

I give him a little confused frown. "Here? You want to dance here?"

"It's a club, right? They do have a dance floor."

I lift an eyebrow toward the BET cameraman. "Nah, I'm good. I'm not in a dancing mood."

"Is he going to be getting in my way for the entire tour?" Sam asks.

"Who?"

Sam jerks his head in the cameraman's direction. "That dude."

"Yeah, probably so. And what do you mean getting in your way? What are you trying to do?"

He shrugs. "I don't know yet. Maybe I'm trying to pick up where we left off."

"I don't know about that, but I do need a road dawg on this tour. I was hoping we'd be cool again by the time we left."

Sam nods slowly. "You already got a road dawg. Your boy Dilly is coming."

"Yeah, I forgot about him. So it looks like I've got two homeboys, right?"

Sam laughs out loud. "Nah, you need a boyfriend, ma. And a roadie. Dilly's the roadie."

"Well, you could be my boyfriend if I could just stop thinking about Rielle. You still with her?"

"I wasn't ever with her, and you already know that. She was my prom date. I'm free as a bird."

"You're free, and I'm free. Look at that."

I like teasing Sam. He deserves it anyway for that whole prom fiasco.

Everyone's eyes go to the DJ booth when Mystique's voice comes over the speakers. "Hey y'all, it's Mystique. I want to wish Ms. Drama a very happy birthday! We're also celebrating the launch of Epsilon Records' summer tour. This next song is the first single from Sunday Tolliver's album. It's called 'Inbox Me.' Hope you like it."

I cringe and want to run and hide somewhere. "Inbox Me" is the only song from my album that I didn't write. Mystique did. It's my least favorite song on the whole record. I only recorded it because I felt like I didn't have a choice. I sure didn't have any say in picking it as a single.

"Why is your face all twisted?" Sam asks. "They're playing your new song! You should be pumped."

I don't respond to Sam because Mystique is walking out of the DJ booth with a huge grin on her face.

"I thought 'Can U See Me' was going to be the first single off my record," I say to Mystique. It's real hard to keep my voice low and my tone free of attitude, but I think I manage to pull it off.

She responds with a huge smile. "It was. Epsilon thought 'Inbox Me' would be more radio friendly. It'll be the follow-up, though."

Either Mystique doesn't see or doesn't care about the stank look on my face. She greets some of her fans, gives some hugs and air kisses, and has Benji hustle her off the dance floor.

I want to continue mean mugging everybody and hightail it to the house, but now, people are congratulating me on my single. The beat is bumping really hard, and it seems kind of weird to hear my own voice blaring out the speakers.

Inbox me / Don't want everyone to know-ow-ow / Inbox me / Get up on this dance floor / Inbox me / Don't leave it on my wall / Inbox me / You don't even have to call. . . .

From the way the club is jumping now, this is sure to be a hit, with Mystique getting paid a grip. Watching the crowd getting pumped and dancing hard off this tune is almost enough to make me be okay with losing a songwriter royalty payout at the end of the day.

Almost.

Suddenly, in the middle of the dance floor, there is a ruckus. I'm nosy, so I crane my neck trying to see what's going on. I still can't see so I move a little closer.

Then the chanting begins.

"Go, Charlie; go, Charlie; go, Charlie; go, Charlie."

It can't be!

OMG, it soooo is my Aunt Charlie, dancing hard on the dance floor! She's grinding on some dude that's got to be young enough to be her son. Her short shorts look extra petite as she dips it low, picks it up slow . . .

I can't believe this is happening.

Clearly, someone has alerted Dreya because she's front and center with extra attitude. She yells something that I can't hear because the music is so loud. Aunt Charlie looks back at her, laughs, and keeps dancing.

Next Dreya loses her mind and tries to snatch Aunt Charlie by the arm. My jaw nearly drops to the floor when Aunt Charlie mugs Dreya in the face and makes her stumble back into the crowd. Then Aunt Charlie goes right back to her new boo!

Dreya tries to lunge again, but Big D is there now, and he picks her up by the waist and carries her off the dance floor.

I don't have to worry about any drama being fabricated about me on our reality show! Dreya and Aunt Charlie are giving enough real-time adventures for a hundred reality shows.

Hot mess'dness to the infinite power.

14

Packing for this tour is not easy, but basically the next six weeks of my life, I'm going to be living out of my suitcase on a tour bus. I'm thinking that I should be more excited than I am.

My mom pops her head into my room. "You ready to go over to the studio?"

"Yep. I think so. If I've forgotten anything, I'll have to get it on the road."

"Okay. Your Aunt Charlie is coming too."

I let out a little chuckle. "Does Dreya know? I don't want her getting all riled up like she did at her party."

My mother shakes her head. "That didn't even make any sense. Charlie was just having fun, trying to celebrate her daughter's birthday."

"Mom. Aunt Charlie is embarrassing! I see why Dreya was mad. I would've been mad if you were doing that!"

My mom puts one hand on her hip and twists her neck

hard. "So you're saying that you don't want me going to the club? I'm grown and so is Charlie."

"I'm not saying that, but Mom, please! Charlie was grinding on a dude. The BET cameras were getting it all on tape."

"And what? Like I said, Charlie is grown. I wish you would think about putting your hands on me like Dreya did Charlie. She owes her mother an apology."

"I would never do that, but I would be just as upset if you were embarrassing me like that."

"Humph! We're just going to have to agree to disagree on this one, I see. Y'all turning eighteen and thinking you can run up on y'all own mamas?"

Aunt Charlie steps into my bedroom as well. As irritating as she is, she looks fly with her weave flipped in the front like how Tiny wears hers. She's got on skinny jeans and a halter, which is nowhere near age-appropriate, but at least she's got the body that she can still rock clothes like that.

"Where you going all dressed up, Charlie?" my mother asks.

"To my BET debut," she replies with a laugh. "My next baby daddy might see me on this show."

My mother laughs out loud. "The last thing you need is another baby."

Manny bursts into my room from the hallway and pushes past his mother to stand in the middle of my bedroom floor. He looks fly too, with his miniature Sean John apparel that Dreya bought him.

"Did I hear my mama say she was havin' a baby?"

Manny asks. "I vote no. I'm the only baby up in this piece."

"Why don't you take your little grown-acting self to the potty before we leave?" my mother says.

"Potty? I don't use the potty, Auntie Shawn. I'm too grown and sexy for that."

My mother smacks him on his behind for his smart mouth, and he runs out of the room—toward the potty. Little man need to stop playing! He can barely aim in the big, grown folk toilet.

"Charlie, you act nice when we get to the studio," my mom warns. "We don't want no mess out of you and Dreya."

"She betta act like she got some sense! She put her hands on me again, I'm gonna beat the tar off her. Think I'm lying? I'm the mother; she's the daughter. She betta recognize."

So it doesn't seem like we're going to have a stress-free episode, at all. I'll just do what I've been doing—make sure I see where the cameraman is pointing and run the opposite direction when the ish hits the fan!

15

The tour bus is enormous! As we pull up to Big D's studio, I take in the huge fifty-five-passenger bus with our faces on the sides! It says EPSILON RECORDS SUMMER TOUR and has me, Dreya, and Truth's promo photos. It also says, SPECIAL GUEST, MYSTIQUE. As far as I know, she's not showing up at any of the concerts. That's probably just a way for her to get more publicity.

According to Big D, Ms. Layla will be in every city with her costumes, but she doesn't ride the bus. Not with a multimillionaire for a daughter. She flies from location to location, even if it's less than an hour away by plane.

I finished my last final—English Lit. And I aced it! Even though I have to miss graduation, I'm officially a graduate! Yeah, baby! My mom is a little bit bummed about me not crossing the stage, but I just reminded her that she'll get to see me graduate from Spelman with honors. Nothing is keeping me from crossing that stage.

The BET camera crew is out in full force! They've added two extra cameras, probably because of everything that popped off last night at the club.

Sam sees us pull up and jogs over to my mom's car. "Hey, Sunday. Are your bags in the trunk?"

"Yep! But you're not a roadie. You're the assistant music director! Let somebody else get the bags."

He grins. "I don't mind getting your bags, Sunday. Roadie or not."

My mother smiles and elbows me before she gets out on her side of the car. "I told you to keep him!"

I shake my head and open my car door. It looks like I'm the last to arrive. Everyone else is already here.

"Why is *she* here?" This is my mother's voice, and it's nearly frantic with anger.

I follow her eyes to see where her glare is going, and then I want to kick myself for not thinking about this. Dilly is standing near the bus with his big sister LaKeisha.

This is all bad.

Before I can stop my mother she's storming over in their direction, and the cameras are trained on her, probably because she looks ready to explode.

My mother bellows, "LaKeisha, you're like a cockroach, always showing up where you're not wanted!"

"Don't be mad, Shawn! Your little songwriter is 'bout to get us all paid," LaKeisha taunts. "Me, Bryce, and Dilly can't wait to start spending the money y'all makin' us."

My mother stops in her tracks, two inches from LaKeisha's face. "Dilly is your brother? What kind of name is that? Sounds like what y'all mama was to keep popping out all this ghetto trash."

Dilly looks like my mother just hit him. She's got a right to be mad at LaKeisha, but dang, why Dilly got to take the wrath too?

"Mom, it's cool," I say when I finally catch up with her. "Dilly's on the label; he's just going along as a roadie."

My mother looks him up and down. "A roadie? Couldn't make the cut, huh? Trying to blow up off of someone else's talent?"

Dilly opens his mouth to say something when LaKeisha interjects, "He's got talent! Way more talent than these two heifers. They're lucky to have him."

Dilly presses his sister back, since the last thing she said was spoken so close to my mother's face, that my mom is wiping LaKeisha's spit off her nose. This is about to get ugly for real.

"Whose picture do you see on the side of this bus, trick? That's my daughter up there!"

LaKeisha laughs. "I don't care who's picture is up there as long as I keep cashing checks."

Aunt Charlie apparently has had enough. She flies past my mother so quickly that no one could stop her if he or she wanted to. She pulls LaKeisha down to the ground by her hair. Or should I say by her weave? And it wasn't in too good either, because a huge section of it tears off in Aunt Charlie's hand.

"My sister can't beat your butt, because she works for the gov'ment," Aunt Charlie says before jumping on LaKeisha. "But I'm about to wipe the street with your ghetto self."

As Big D and Sam pull my Aunt Charlie off of LaKeisha, I can hear her laughing. She spits at Aunt Charlie, and misses. She better be glad too, because not even Big D could've held her back if any of that saliva had gotten in Aunt Charlie's premium Indian Remy hair.

"You and your sister are gutter rats," LaKeisha says. "I'm 'bout to be out of here."

She slowly gets up and wipes the dirt off her clothing and smoothes down her hair. Dilly stands frozen, as if he doesn't know what to do. I'm sure he wants to help his sister, but he's about to get on a tour bus with us. He's not trying to mess up his big break over their drama. I don't blame him.

"This ain't ova, Charlie," LaKeisha says as she stumbles toward her car.

"What, you and your fake gangsta brother gonna come and shoot me too? Try it and both of y'all gonna be up under the jail."

My mother says, "Charlie. That's enough." She narrows her eyes and glares in LaKeisha's direction even after her car has pulled off. Then she gives Dilly the most evil-looking face that I've ever seen her give anyone. That's so not fair. He hasn't done anything.

"Mom, I meant to tell you . . ."

She gives me the hand, and says, "Sunday, don't even. I can't believe you would put yourself and your family in harm's way by going to prom with him. LaKeisha and Bryce's brother?"

"Mommy, I'm sorry. I didn't tell you because I thought you'd be angry."

"I'm beyond angry, Sunday. I'm hurt. You know how they hurt me with what they did to Carlos."

"But that wasn't Dilly! He didn't pull the trigger."

My mother shakes her head in disgust. "You can thank yourself if something else goes down."

I watch speechlessly as my mother, Aunt Charlie, and a sobbing Manny go back to the car.

I feel a troubling sadness overwhelm me. I never meant to upset my mom like this. That's just all bad. Plus, I was trying to stay out of the spotlight. Now, I'm front and dead center. Dreya and Aunt Charlie's fight at the club pales in comparison to this.

I'm starting to think that being immortalized on film is never a good thing.

16

While we're on the road to Birmingham, Alabama, for our first show, everyone is giving me my space. Even Dreya, who would usually find a reason to capitalize off my embarrassment, is laying off the wisecracks.

This tour bus is tricked all the way out! The seats are soft and spacious, and when you recline them, it feels just like a bed. There's a mini kitchen in the back with a microwave and an oven. I wonder if we would've got this fab life treatment if the BET cameras weren't on the road with us.

I'm sitting here listening to Lauryn Hill on my iPod. Her melancholy voice is matching my sour mood, but her lyrics are soothing my spirit.

After singing along quietly to "Can't Take My Eyes Off of You," I look up and see Dilly standing in the aisle next to my seat.

I pull the earbuds out of my ears. "What's up?"

"Can I sit down next to you?" he asks. "I don't necessarily want the whole bus to hear our conversation."

I scoot over next to the window and let Dilly have a seat. "You look like you've got something on your mind," I say.

"I just want you to know that I'm not trying to have a come up off of you."

"I don't even think that, Dilly, and my mother doesn't either."

Dilly sucks his teeth and pokes out his lips. "Yeah, right. Your mother hates my guts, and she doesn't even know me."

I don't even know why Dilly is going here. He knows what's really good concerning that shooting, so I know he's not gonna try to sit up here and act like my mom is the villain of this episode.

"Dilly, don't play. You know why my mom has beef with your siblings. Don't make me put it out there like that while we've got a whole television crew on this bus recording our every word."

He sighs. "I know what y'all think went down, and like I told you before, you don't know the entire story."

"I'm sure neither of us do, so I don't think we should be taking sides," I reply in a calmer tone.

"But you have taken sides, right? You've taken Carlos's side."

I think about Carlos standing in my bedroom looking like an escaped convict, and I can't help but feel some pity for him. Whatever went down between him and Bryce is irrelevant. Bryce is walking the streets free to do whatever, and Carlos is living hand to mouth.

I place my hand over Dilly's hand. "Weren't you the one who told me that their drama didn't have anything to do with us? Let's just have fun on this tour and worry about all that when we get home."

He looks up at me and almost mesmerizes me with those big eyes and long lashes. "As long as you're cool, I'm cool."

"I'm cool, boy. Now let me listen to my music."

Dilly gives me one last smile before he gets up and goes back to his seat. I think he's optimistic about us being friends, and maybe hopeful that we'll be more than friends. But when I think about the look on my mother's face when she saw LaKeisha, I can't be sure of either one. I'm all about collabos and making paper, but breaking my mother's heart is not on my agenda.

17

Tonight is our first show in Birmingham, Alabama, and I'm a ball of nerves. You would think this was my first time ever performing! I'm having fears that I'll forget the words to my songs, forget the dance steps, or worse, slip and fall on my butt trying to do Mystique's complicated moves.

The BET camera crew is set up backstage to record all of our pre-concert activities, and everyone is doing their usual pre-show routine. Truth is in the corner mumbling lyrics and drinking lukewarm water. Dreya is making demands and sipping out of a can of Sprite. I'm doing breathing exercises trying to calm my jitters.

Ms. Layla just got here and is directing a small crew around several racks of clothing. It's just one show, so I don't know why she has all this inventory here. It's like she wants to have a backup outfit, and a backup for the backup, and a backup for the backup's backup. Just ridiculous if you ask me.

Since I'm performing first, she starts holding pieces up to me and either shaking her head or nodding and smiling. I've already tried all of this stuff on, so I don't know why she can't just hand me something.

"How are you feeling tonight, Sunday? Are you feeling positive energy or negative energy?" Ms. Layla asks.

I lift one eyebrow and shrug. How am I even supposed to answer that question? She takes my wrist and taps it about twenty times.

"There, that's better. Your aura is brighter now."

Okay . . . um . . . yeah.

I don't think Dreya likes me getting attended to first, because she storms over to Ms. Layla's racks of clothing.

"Where is my outfit?" Dreya asks. "I need to see what I'm supposed to be wearing, because I might need to make some changes."

Ms. Layla drops my wrist and slowly turns toward Dreya. She gives her an up and down look. "Your aura is dark; pick something black from over there."

Ms. Layla waves at the far rack and goes back to picking out my outfit.

Dreya fusses, "I can't find anything on these messy hangers! Someone needs to help me immediately. Sunday can wear anything. She's the opening act. I'm one of the headliners."

Ms. Layla sighs and says, "Sunday, please excuse me. I'll be right back in a few moments. Take some deep breaths. Inhale deeply; exhale slowly. You seem nervous; your heart is racing. Find your center."

Find my center? What is this? Am I the Karate Kid, and she's Ms. Miyagi? But, maybe there is something to this, because the breathing *is* helping, and I definitely didn't tell her about my feeling nervous.

I watch Ms. Layla quickly put together an ensemble that Dreya approves. It reminds me of a black spacesuit. Actually, it looks like Michael Jackson's "Beat It" jacket, but as a bodysuit. Yes, attempt to visualize that with me.

Ms. Layla comes back and hands me a half T-shirt and a pair of cargo jeans. She strokes her chin like she's thinking and decides to finish off the outfit with a black baseball cap with HOT GIRL spelled out in rhinestones.

"Put on those Converse sneakers with the outfit," Ms. Layla says. "I don't want you trying to dance in heels on your first time out."

Thank you! Thank you! Thank you!

Now I have to find somewhere to put all this on. We've got shared dressing rooms, even though Dreya pitched a fit about wanting her own. The guys have one, and the girls have one. Dancers, singers, roadies, and everybody else has to use the same dressing area.

Since the girls' dressing room has been taken over by Dreya and a few dancers, I try to find some other corner or closet that might be acceptable. As much room as there is backstage, I can say that there aren't many hiding places.

Just as I'm about to give up and squeeze in with Dreya, I see what looks like a broom closet. I hope it's unlocked, because it's perfect. It's off in the cut and way backstage in a poorly lit corner. No BET cameras back here either. It's exactly what I'm looking for.

I look over both shoulders to make sure no one has followed me, and then I rush to the door and open it without knocking.

I should've knocked.

My jaw drops open when I see Bethany and Truth liplocked and tongue kissing in the closet. I feel like I'm totally on pause, because I don't know if I should close the door back or say, "Gotcha!"

Finally, Bethany is the one who moves. She pushes Truth off of her and runs out of the closet with a mortified look on her face. Truth just gives me a sheepish grin, like I'm supposed to be cool with this.

"You're tripping, you know that, right?" I ask.

"I'm just doing me. Your girl's been hounding me since day one. I'm just giving her what she wants."

If I didn't have to perform in less than fifteen minutes, I would probably fight him right now. And of course, there are no cameras anywhere around catching this ratchedness on film! They catch my mama about to come to blows with a murderer's sister, but Truth being the dog that he is, gets absolutely no airplay.

Truth wipes his mouth with the back of his hand and strides away.

"Make sure you get that glitter lip gloss off your neck," I call as he walks away.

He looks back over his shoulder at me and laughs. This is so not a laughing matter. And why did I have to see it? Why can't I be blissfully ignorant? Why I gotta be all up in the mix?

No, thank you.

But right now, I don't have time to think about Truth, Bethany, and their ratchedness. I have to get ready to go on stage, and sing for my fans. We're releasing "Can U See Me" and "Inbox Me" on iTunes tomorrow. Mystique thought it would be hot if we put them out on the same day.

Personally, I think she observed how heated I was about "Inbox Me" being my first single, and she wanted to keep the peace. Or maybe she doesn't care about keeping the peace with me, because I'm just an artist and she's the grand diva of Epsilon Records. Whatever the reason, I'm just glad I'm going to see some songwriter payout on my royalty statement.

That's what's up.

Finally I'm dressed, and I head back toward the stage area. The stage crew is walking around shouting orders, and Dilly takes my hand and leads me to where I need to stand behind the stage.

"Are you ready?" he asks.

"Yeah, I think so." I do some more of Ms. Layla's deep, cleansing breaths to help me get my mind right.

"I'll let you know when you need to go out on stage," Dilly says. "It won't be long now, less than five minutes."

Big D walks up to us and gives me a bear hug. "All right, my little platinum prodigy! Go out there and make your big brother proud!"

"That's a lot of pressure, Big D," I say with a chuckle. "I really didn't need that right now. Ms. Layla said my aura is cloudy or something."

He laughs out loud. "Cloudy? Nah, never that. You're a star, baby girl."

I like this. Love it in fact. There's no better way to get me pumped than to tell me I'm a star. That's called positive reinforcement. Know what I mean?

I can't really hear what's going on out on the stage. All I can hear is loud noise and applause. We've got a sellout audience. Okay, so what if the tickets were only ten dollars and the venue only holds three thousand people? A sellout crowd is a sellout crowd in my book.

Dilly hears something in his headset, taps me on the arm, and nods. "It's time, Sunday. Just do what you do best."

I start to run out on stage, and Dilly grabs me. "Your microphone!"

He switches on my wireless microphone, and I run out on the stage. As soon as I hear the music, I get pumped and forget all about my nerves.

The first song I perform is "Can U See Me." I don't know how some of the crowd knows the words since it has yet to be released, but when they start singing the chorus with me, I feel a total rush!

I messed up a couple of times on the choreography, but I don't think anyone noticed. At least I didn't fall on my butt!

When my set is finished, all of a sudden I'm dog tired! But the screaming crowd and their chant of "Sun-day! Sun-day!" was so worth it.

I run off stage with all of the dancers. They rush to change clothes for Dreya's set, but I'm stopped by the BET cameras.

"How do you feel?" the cameraman asks.

"I feel totally drained! My adrenaline was all the way up out there. Now, I think I'm crashing!"

"Did you enjoy the performance?" he asks.

I nod as I take a swig of water from the bottle Dilly hands me. "This is hands down, one of the best nights of my life. I can't believe that this is happening to me!"

As the words come out of my mouth, I see Bethany staring at me from a corner. She's giving me a look that's a mixture of hatred, jealousy, and sadness.

My mind flashes back to her and Truth slobbering each other down, and my heart feels heavy. Bethany was always one of us. She was part of Daddy's Little Girls.

Now, it's Dreya's turn to start her set.

"Wish me luck," she says to Bethany, who has now come closer.

Bethany swallows and says, "Break a leg."

Bethany doesn't say this with any malice, per se, but there is an undertone of negativity. I don't think Dreya caught it, and maybe I wouldn't have either if I hadn't seen Bethany sucking face with Truth.

Everything in Dreya's set starts off fine! She's doing her thing. Her gyrating, half-singing, booty-popping thing that she does best.

I'm watching from backstage, and the crowd is eating it up. Every time she dips to the floor the guys roar, and every time she yells "Where my ladies at?" she gets a round of applause.

"Does Birmingham like dem dirty south girls?" Dreya asks.

The audience chants her lyrics back to her. "We like dem dirty, dirty, dirty south girls!"

She sings, "Come on tell me fellas, do you like them dirty south girls?"

Truth runs out from backstage and chants with the guys, "Them dirty, dirty south girls is what we like!"

The crowd roars again with thunderous applause when they see Truth. Dreya launches into her verses, and she starts off doing well.

Then . . . the unthinkable occurs.

Her track, the one she's lip-synching to, skips to the hook of the song. It's obvious to the crowd that she's not singing live, and a few of them start to boo. She tries to recover and launch into the hook, but the booing gets a little louder.

Truth gets on the microphone and says, "Come on y'all! This my girl up here!"

I guess this works because the boos die down, and Dreya can sing again. I can tell she's rattled, though. Her voice is shaking, and she's stumbling through her dance moves.

When she finally seems to get back into the swing of things on her duet with Truth, "Love Is," another ridiculous snafu happens! She grabs the microphone and stomps one of her feet, and the heel on her boot breaks!

Luckily, she doesn't fall, and she makes the best out of the situation. She bends over and slowly unzips the boot, to screams and yells from the guys, and tosses it to the side of the stage. She does the same for the other boot. When she's done with the song, Truth calls some stage hands out. They carry Dreya off the stage with her legs outstretched and blowing kisses like a true diva.

As soon as they set her down outside the stage area, Dreya spontaneously combusts. She yells profanities at all of the stage hands, and calls them names. The BET camera guy is gonna have plenty of bleeping out to do on this reel before it's fit for TV.

Ms. Layla strolls over when she hears Dreya screaming her name. "You're making a fool of yourself," Ms. Layla says. "It could've happened to anyone."

Did I just see Dreya's head spin around?

"I'm making a fool of myself?" Dreya asks. "I think you sabotaged me. You gave me that broken boot on purpose."

"I would never do such a thing. That would only hurt my reputation as a concert stylist. You should be more concerned about learning to sing live so that you don't need a track."

Dreya explodes again. "You don't tell me what I need to be concerned about! You better be concerned about getting me some boots that aren't cheap, and won't break on stage. Or I'll ruin you! You hear me? I'll ruin you."

To this Ms. Layla throws her head back and laughs. "Honey, you don't have the power to ruin me yet. Come and say that to me once you've done more than lip-synch to a track and shake your behind."

Ms. Layla strides away leaving Dreya with no comeback at all. I guess Ms. Layla told her! Dreya better recognize. Ms. Layla is old school, and her daughter runs this industry.

Dreya seems to be irritated that all of us are staring at

her in shock. She straightens her back, and blinks a few times. I know it's to keep back the tears.

She yells, "Where is Bethany?"

Bethany makes herself immediately available. She runs up with a pair of shoes for Dreya to put on her stockinged feet.

"Thank you, girl. At least somebody here has my back."

Bethany glances at me and swallows hard. "You know I ride or die for you, Drama."

Wow. Phony on top of phony. I almost want to give Bethany a round of applause for her Academy Award-winning performance. But the uncomfortable look on her face keeps me from doing anything that might give away her true intentions.

For a fleeting instant, I wish things were like they used to be, with me, Dreya, and Bethany singing harmonies in the living room and making up dance steps in the garage. But things aren't like they used to be anymore, and I haven't the slightest idea how to get it back.

18

After the concert, the entire crew goes to Applebee's for dinner. Of course the cameras are here to catch all of us looking tired and grumpy. The high from the concert has worn off, and I think we're all pretty irritable, but no one more than Dreya.

She's sitting at a table with Truth, still wearing her stage makeup because she wouldn't let anyone touch her. She's convinced that we're all out to destroy her. Everyone but the two who are betraying her the most—Truth and Bethany.

Sam sits at a table with me, Big D, our makeup artist Regina, Shelly, and Bethany. Dilly's with the stage crew because that's where Big D told him to sit. Big D doesn't want more drama for us when we get back to Atlanta, so he's trying his best to minimize Dilly's screen time on our reality show. I dig him for that. Big D is looking out for us and for his pocketbook at the same time. Can't be mad at that.

"You had a great show, Sunday," Sam says. "Every time I see you on stage, I can't believe that I actually know you. You kind of transform out there."

I give him a beaming smile in response. I can't tell if he's doing this for the cameras or if he's for real. I'm hoping it's for real, because that's a heck of a compliment to get from a guy you kind of like.

Sam is wearing some kind of cologne that smells great and tickles my nose. He's not wearing his signature spectacles tonight—he's au naturel. He's wearing an Epsilon Summer Tour T-shirt and some distressed jeans.

Shelly says, "I'm so proud of you, Sunday! I remember that first day you was up at the studio eating up everything in sight. You came downstairs and busted out that hook! I knew you were gonna be a celebrity."

"Thanks, Shelly. I believe you when you say it."

Sam looks stricken, "You don't believe me?"

"Oh, stop acting, thirsty boy," Regina says. "She believes you too."

"Jacksonville Beach is next," Big D says. "You ready for the next show?"

I sigh. "Do we get a break at all?"

"We'll get to the hotel in the morning probably. Y'all perform that evening on the beach, so you'll have the whole day to get some rest."

"Dang!" I exclaim. "Y'all trying to kill me."

Big D bursts into laughter. "Girl, you're eighteen years

old. If you can't do this now, you'll never hang in the business. You should be at your peak performance physically."

"I guess," I mumble.

"Can you hang?" he asks.

"Yeah. I can hang."

Sam looks across the room at something, and his eyes light up. He starts humming, "Bummm, bum, bum, bum, bummmm, bummmm. Bummmm, bum, bum, bum, bummmmm."

It's the tune to the graduation march! I turn around and see the Applebee's waiters and waitresses bringing over a dessert with a candle in it.

When I look back at Sam, he's whipped out a graduation cap and tassel! He reaches across the table and places it on my head. Not only did he get the right color (royal blue), but he also remembered my National Honor Society gold tassel.

Big D grins at me as tears fill my eyes. He hands me my diploma and says, "The principal at Decatur High, Ms. Washburn, wanted me to congratulate you on your graduation. And she wants you to accept this diploma, and wishes you good luck in college!"

Big D hands Bethany her diploma as well, "Congratulations, Bethany. Thanks for being a part of the Epsilon crew."

She smiles and says, "Thanks, Big D!"

I'm waiting for Big D to get up and hand Dreya a diploma too. But this doesn't happen. Of course, she storms over to the table looking crazy.

"Where is my diploma, Big D? I'm sick of y'all playing me tonight."

"Well, Drama, this celebration was supposed to be for all three of y'all, but unfortunately . . ."

"Unfortunately *what?*" Dreya asks.

"You didn't graduate, ma. You're a half credit short in English. You didn't pass your final exam."

"That's a lie!" Dreya wailed. "Bethany and I used the same . . . study guide."

Bethany looks away with a guilty expression on her face. I know what this means. I've seen that look before. Bethany and Dreya are professional cheaters. Their code word for cheat sheet is "study guide." That way they can fool my mom.

Usually, Bethany provides the "study guides" that she gets from a friend. Dreya lived and died by those cheat sheets, because it would never occur to her to actually study for a test. But it is interesting that Bethany passed the test and graduated and Dreya did not.

Did Bethany not cheat?

Or did she give Dreya a fake cheat sheet?

If it's the latter, then Bethany is on some fouler stuff than I thought she was. This whole jealousy thing is getting deep.

"I didn't need that study guide, Dreya. I had my own notes," Bethany says after taking too long a pause before responding.

Dreya narrows her eyes, and a dark shadow seems to pass over her face. "Guess I should've studied harder. I'll make it up with my tutor after the tour."

"That's right," Big D says. "You don't have a choice, ma. No diploma, no recording contract."

Dreya rolls her eyes at Big D and sashays back over to

her private table with Truth. It looks like he attempts to console Dreya by giving her a hug, but she shrugs him off and plops down at the table.

Bethany asks, "This was almost as good as crossing the stage, right, Sunday?"

"Ummmm . . . not really! But I wouldn't trade this night for anything. The energy that the crowd had was off the chain. I hope that the rest of the crowds are like that."

"You keep singing like you do, and they will be," Big D says.

Dilly strides over to our table, with a grin on his face. Big D looks annoyed, but he doesn't send him away.

"Hey, Sunday, I heard you graduated. Since you showed me off at your prom, I just wanted to congratulate you."

"Thanks, Dilly."

Dilly then turns his attention to Bethany. "Congratulations to you too, girl. Looks like we're the only ones on this tour not coupled up, so maybe we can hang out a little bit in our down time."

"Y'all ain't the only ones not coupled up," I say quickly. Too quickly if you judge by the evil expression on Sam's face.

"Oh, do you want me to holla at you, Sunday?" Dilly asks.

"Naw. I just want you to know that you're not alone. You don't have to feel pressured to have a boo out here."

Sam chimes in. "Right. Sunday doesn't know much about coupling up."

Sam looks annoyed beyond belief as I give him a "what did I do" expression. I know exactly what I did, but I had to do it. I don't want Dilly chasing after Bethany. She's beyond used goods. And plus, she's already got one *boo* on this tour. No need for her to hog all the guys.

Dilly locks eyes with Big D, and I guess he decides that his time is up. "I'ma let y'all enjoy your food."

"Yeah, thanks," Sam says.

Sam gives Dilly a little shooing motion with his hand, dismissing him from the table. Now, he knows he's dead wrong for that. Dilly doesn't deserve that.

Dilly acts like the bigger man and doesn't retaliate. He walks back over to his crew without saying another word.

I poke my lips out at Sam and flare my nose angrily. "You wrong," I say.

"What?"

Big D, Regina, and Shelly start laughing. When Sam and Bethany join in too, I can't help but chuckle a little bit. I swallow that jovial activity, however, when I catch a glimpse of Dilly. He looks hurt, like he thinks we're laughing at him.

"Congratulations again, baby girl," Sam says. "Spelman ain't ready for you."

I decide to drop my irritation for now. "I know, right! Where are you going to college, Bethany?"

She laughs. "I don't know. I'm thinking Georgia Tech. I tried to get into Spelman, but I guess I didn't make the cut."

You dang skippy Bethany didn't make the cut. I want to laugh out loud. I'd be surprised if she got into any school with her C- average, spotty attendance, and lack of extracurricular activities. I think what she's doing now is exactly what she'll be doing next year: Kissing Dreya's behind and stealing Dreya's boyfriend.

19

We got to our Jacksonville Beach hotel at eight o'clock in the morning after driving all night long. I'm not as tired as I thought I'd be, because I slept the entire way. After we checked in, Sam and I decided to have a late breakfast in the hotel lobby.

He looks a little bit sleepy as he whips his spoon around in a bowl of grits. "So, I asked Big D about the royalty statements."

"You did!" I perk up. "What did he say? When do I get paid?"

"He said that Epsilon Records pays quarterly, and the next payment is in September."

"So, I'll get a check in September?"

"Actually, no. Your album doesn't drop until the first week of July, and your singles drop today. The September payment is for March, April, and May."

I give Sam a blank stare.

Sam continues, "The good news is that you'll get a check at the end of the tour. It'll be your pay from the tour."

"I just want them to rush me all my money. I should get paid as soon as they get paid."

Sam laughs, "And what? Keep the record company from making interest off of all the money they get from your record sales?"

"Sounds too much like right, doesn't it?" I ask.

Sam laughs out loud. "At least you've got songwriter credit coming on your statement. Your cousin is going to be really surprised when she sees her royalty payout. If she has one."

"I know. I tried to tell her, but she doesn't listen to me. I tried to tell Aunt Charlie too. She just said that she was looking for a Hollywood agent for Dreya so that she can get endorsements and movie cameos."

Sam cocks his head to one side as if in thought. "That's not a bad idea. After the show comes on BET, all of y'all will be stars."

"Like I said, I don't care about all that. I just want them to rush me my benjis. Know what I mean?"

"Yeah, I know what you mean."

Sam steals a piece of my French toast. It really is good, and they gave me two small pieces. He better be glad I like him, because I'd be going upside his head for eating out of my plate.

After he swallows, he says, "You don't have cooties, do you?"

"No!" I say with a laugh. "But speaking of which, did you know that Truth is messing with Bethany?"

Sam holds his stomach and cracks up. "How is that revelation related to cooties? Are you saying Bethany has them or Truth?"

"Probably both of them! That's what I was talking about at Applebee's! I don't want Dilly to get all into Bethany, and she's creeping with Truth."

Tears fall from Sam's eyes from laughing so hard. When he finally catches his breath, he says, "Yeah, I knew he was messing around with her. He likes playing with fire, I guess. If Drama finds out about that, it's gonna be crazy."

Crazy is not quite the word I'm looking for.

More like catastrophic.

20

After my breakfast with Sam, I do start to feel a little bit sleepy. I guess that's what grits, French toast, scrambled eggs with cheese, and bacon will do to you. All that food is sitting in my stomach and begging me to take a nap.

I kick off my sandals and wiggle my toes. Then, I plop down on the bed on my back. I don't turn down the covers yet; I'm just resting my eyes for right now.

As I'm drifting off to dreamland, I hear a knock on my hotel room door. I almost don't get up to open it, but then I decide that whoever it is will just keep knocking and I'll get even more irritated.

I swing the door open, and Bethany is standing there, looking more nervous than a mug. I step to the side and usher her in. Something tells me this is going to be a conversation that needs to happen behind closed doors.

"Are you going to tell Dreya about me and Truth?"

"How about this? What if I help you with your career? Then, you could leave Truth alone, and nobody gets hurt."

"You would do that for me?" Bethany asks with a hopeful tone in her voice.

"No. I'd do it for my cousin, though."

Bethany's face wrinkles from its pleasant expression to a frown. "Why would you do anything to keep her from hurting? She hates your guts. She was so mad that your performance went well last night."

I sigh and shrug. "Even if she doesn't act right, she's still my cousin. That's what we do in our family."

"Yeah, well, whatever. How are you going to help me get a record deal?"

I don't like the way her voice sounds right now. It's almost like she's got this little entitlement thing going, where somebody *has* to help her. She's got it twisted.

"Me and Sam will write you a few songs and record a demo for you when we get back home. You're already around the people who can make it happen, so if you've got any potential, Mystique or even Big D will jump right on it.

Bethany shakes her head. "I don't want to work with Big D. He can't make any decisions on anything without going through Epsilon Records. I want to work with Mystique."

I feel myself getting impatient with this conversation. I mean like, dang! You give some people an inch.

"We'll see what Mystique says," I reply. "But I'm not going to make any promises. Just like Truth couldn't make you any promises either. No matter what he told you."

"Okay, then. That's what's up."

"I'm telling you right now, though, if I find out you still messing with Truth, the deal is off, and I'm telling Dreya what you're doing."

"You don't have to worry about that. I'm done with him. He's a lowlife anyway. Plus, I think Dilly might want to holler at me."

"What about Romell? Are you done with him, too?"

Bethany laughs out loud. "Did you really think I was gonna holla at him after high school? Negative!"

I keep quiet on this one. I don't know why Dilly tried to holla at Bethany at Applebee's last night. I kind of got the feeling that he was trying to make me jealous. But I'm not sure. He might really be feeling her.

I do know that if Bethany keeps it up with Truth, she's not going to like the outcome at the end of the day.

"Bethany, can I ask you a question?"

"Yeah," she replies.

"Would you do *anything* for a record deal? You're just putting yourself out there, and it seems a little crazy if you ask me."

She takes a few long moments before she responds. "I wouldn't do *anything* for a record deal. I wouldn't get hooked on drugs or prostitute myself out or anything like that."

"But anything else is like fair game?"

She gives a sad chuckle. "Yeah, pretty much. I want fame, and I want the money. I'm not trying to be broke down in some raggedy part of Atlanta for the rest of my life."

"Yeah, I get all that. But you seem like you're giving up everything, even your friends!"

"I gotta do what I gotta do."

"Is it worth your soul?"

Bethany doesn't give a reply to this question. She gives a heavy-sounding sigh and walks toward my hotel room door.

"I'll talk to you later, Sunday. Get some rest; you've got a show later. Looking forward to working with you on my demo."

She closes the door, and I lie back down on my bed with a heavy heart. It's crazy the things that some people will do for the fab life. Bethany thinks she's on the way to superstar status, but if you ask me she's making all the wrong moves.

21

Performing on the beach might seem like a really cool thing to do as an artist. But when it's ninety degrees in the shade and the sun is blazing down on your head, you might have a totally different opinion about it. Especially when the cool waves are crashing against the shore, and you're drenched in sweat.

If you haven't already guessed, I'm ridiculously hot, and I haven't even started performing yet. One of the veejays from *106 and Park* is here hosting the concert live as part of a *Summer Splash* special, and she's out there getting the crowd pumped. I appreciate her for that, but I'd really appreciate getting this over with.

To distract myself from the heat, I watch the little dramedy going on between Dreya and Ms. Layla. Dreya is refusing to wear any of Ms. Layla's outfits after the wardrobe malfunction in Birmingham.

"I'm not wearing that hot-looking catsuit. You've got

me messed up. This stuff looks like somebody bought it at Rave!" Dreya shouts. "This is not couture."

"How many times do I have to say that you either wear my clothing on stage or you go on naked?" Ms. Layla asks. "There is no other stylist for this concert."

Big D does the necessary and intervenes. "Listen, Drama, you have to compromise."

"It's a hundred degrees out here. I'm not wearing this spandex mess."

Big D nods. "I can understand that. Ms. Layla, can we get her something a little less suffocating for this show? It is a beach party."

"It's not a full catsuit," Ms. Layla explains. "She would know that if she'd tried it on. There's more sheer material and cutouts than spandex. It breathes, and it wouldn't be hot at all."

"How about something casual?" Big D asks. "Like a bathing suit top and cutoff shorts or something?"

Ms. Layla sighs. "Y'all know nothing about styling a concert. That's something I would give Sunday to wear. It fits her image. Drama has spent all this time creating an edgy persona, and now you want me to give her girl-next-door clothes?"

Dreya fingers the catsuit monstrosity. She holds it up and looks at the sheer pieces and cutouts. Then, she holds it up to her body, while Big D and Ms. Layla keep arguing.

"Ms. Layla, I just want everyone to be happy. I want you to be happy, because you know I love you and Mystique. But I also want the artists to be happy. If they're not happy, they are not performing at their full potential, and that messes up my money."

"Well, you need to explain to Drama how all of this works. She doesn't seem to understand what it means to have a contract."

Dreya clears her throat, and Big D and Ms. Layla look at her. "I'll wear this," she says. "It'll do for this once. From now on, I want the right to approve or veto any outfits you think I might wear."

Dreya carries the catsuit off to her makeshift booth behind the stage, leaving Big D and Ms. Layla looking dumbfounded.

Bethany walks up to me with an irritated look on her face. She was watching the action too.

"Drama is tripping. Why would she take them through all that if she was just going to put the outfit on?"

I laugh out loud. "Because she's Dreya. And because the cameras are rolling."

I think that Dreya has decided to own this role of difficult diva. Maybe she thinks it'll make her the star of the show, like NeNe Leakes on *The Real Housewives*. It's whatever! Better her than me.

Dilly walks up and asks, "Can I attach your microphone to your top?"

"Yes. Let's get this over with, so I can perform."

Dilly slides his hand under the strap on my halter top. I feel a little shiver go through me from the skin on skin contact.

"Sorry," he says. "I didn't mean to molest you. I just had to put this on the right way."

I laugh out loud. "I don't feel molested."

"You look tired, Sunday," Dilly says as he cocks his head to one side and examines my face. "Aren't you pumped to perform?"

"Honestly, I wish I could just fast forward this part. I don't know if you can tell, but I have a touch of stage fright."

"You do? You sure hide it well."

I take in a deep breath and let it out slowly. Clearing out my auras, because I'm sure if they weren't cloudy yesterday, they sure are now.

"You're on, Sunday," Dilly says as he hears the intro to my first song.

I jog out onto the stage and look out at the crowd. They're extra pumped because they're on TV, and because there are no chairs, everyone is standing up and dancing. It's a real party atmosphere that kind of takes me back to when I first started singing with Dreya and Bethany. We'd do little performances at people's parties, and everyone thought we were the bomb.

I hear the intro fade out, and I start singing. Immediately, I can tell something is not right. I can hear me singing, but the microphone is out. Only the people at the edge of the stage can hear me, and the people in the back are starting to grumble.

I hold up one hand to cue the band, and they seem to get the drift. They go into the breakdown part of the song. The backup singers sing their little piece, while Dilly runs out on stage with a handheld microphone.

"Hey y'all," I say to the crowd. "Seem like we having

a little bit of technical difficulty tonight. Y'all ready to party?"

The crowd yells, "Yeah!"

"Thank you for the microphone, Dilly. Y'all give Dilly a round of applause."

The crowd cheers and claps for Dilly. He beams at me, and I give him a wink and a smile.

"Hey, y'all don't know about Dilly yet, but he's one of the hottest rappers coming out of this camp, no doubt. Y'all want him to freestyle for y'all?"

Again, the crowd cheers, "Yeah!!!"

I hand Dilly the microphone, and he chuckles. "How she gone put a brotha on the spot? Give me a good beat."

Dilly motions to the band, and they give him the beginning of one of his tracks. "Look at Sunday Tolliver / think I'ma try to conquer her. / She so popular. / On Twitter I'm her follower. / Think I'd drop all them chicks for her. / Think I could get love sick for her. / If I could only just get her / to kick her lame dude to the curb."

The applause roars when Dilly hands me the microphone back. He takes a deep bow, and I giggle as he winks at me again. Sam is gonna be salty, but he'll get over it. That freestyle was hotness.

"Give it up for Dilly!" I say, as the band starts the intro to "Inbox Me."

I get through the rest of my set incident free. Actually, I think I perform better because Dilly helped loosen me and the crowd up. That's what's up.

When I get backstage Sam is waiting for me. "Y'all real cute, you know that?" he says.

"He's just joking. Plus, you and I are not officially together anyway. He could've been talking about anyone."

"Yeah, but he was talking about me."

I stroke Sam's cheek. "Don't get mad. He didn't mean it."

"So do you want to get out of here?"

"What, like now?" I ask. "Big D would trip if I leave before the show is over."

"Nah, he's cool with it. I told him you were looking tired, and he said if anyone asked about you he'd say you'd gone to lie down."

"Where are we going? Back to the hotel?"

He nods. "The hotel has a spa with its own private pool and hot tub. I thought we could hang out there. No one will know where we are."

"Are you gonna try something, Sam? You know I took a basic self-defense class, right? I do know how to put you in a submission hold."

Sam laughs out loud. "A submission hold? You don't need to worry about that. I just want to hang out with my friend. Is that okay?"

Sam and I sneak out of the concert area and back to our hotel rooms to change. I put on a very modest one-piece swimming suit. I don't want Sam getting all twisted. Plus, this is a friend outing.

He meets me outside my hotel room, and we take an elevator to the hotel's penthouse floor. The doors open to a beautiful and peaceful-looking spa. There are palm trees, and some kind of lemon scented mist is blowing through the air. It's like an indoor rainforest.

"This is niiiice," I whisper. I feel crazy talking out loud, because it's so quiet.

"I know, right. Do you want a spa service? A massage or something like that?"

I scrunch my eyebrows together. "Um, how much is that?"

"You are cheap, Sunday!" Sam says with a laugh. "It's only eighty bucks."

"Eighty bucks! I ain't gonna be able to do that."

"I'll pay for it, even though you can afford it."

I shake my head adamantly. "No, you won't. Let's get in the hot tub. That'll be just as good as a massage."

Sam races me over to the huge hot tub. He beats me in and eases into the hot water. I can tell by his facial expression that he got in too fast.

I ease myself in. "Ooh, that feels good," I say.

I didn't realize how sore and tired I was until the hot water caressed my body and soothed my achy muscles.

Sam asks, "You excited about college? It's just around the corner."

"Yeah, I am, but I haven't been able to think about it much with this tour and record deal going on."

"I know. We've been more busy than the average high school graduates. But I can't wait to hit that college campus."

"No doubt. But it's a good kind of busy, because we're making money."

"That we are. Are you gonna live on campus at Spelman or are you getting an apartment?"

"I couldn't get one if I wanted to. Freshmen have to live on campus."

Sam slides down the wall so that he's up to his neck in the water. "I'm sure they'd make an exception for you. You're a celebrity."

"I'm not a celebrity yet."

"You will be soon. Can you imagine what it would be like as a platinum-selling artist pledging a sorority?"

I scrunch my nose up. I don't like the idea at all. "Sorority? I don't know if I'm a sorority kind of girl."

"You've got to go Greek! And old school too. You're a Delta all day and all night."

"I am? I thought I was more of an AKA?"

Sam shakes his head. "Either are good, but since I'm going to be an Omega man, you should pledge Delta."

"And why would I want to do that?"

"Because we're going to be college sweethearts."

I toss my head back and bathe my neck and hair in the water. "We are?"

"Yeah. Don't you think so?"

I chuckle. "No comment. What else do you want to do at Georgia Tech other than join a fraternity?"

Sam rolls his eyes. Probably because I evaded his question. He'll get over it.

"I think I'm trying out for the marching band," he says.

"Marching band? What band instrument do you play?"

Sam makes a drumming motion with his hands as if he's holding invisible drum sticks. "Snare drum."

"You're a little drummer boy? I didn't know that."

Sam smiles, and immediately his face is two hundred percent cuter than it normally is. "There are a lot of things you don't know about me."

"Okay, I'll accept that. We really haven't gotten to

know each other outside of music. I've gotta admit I thought you were a little shallow."

Sam's eyes buck out of his head. "Shallow? Are you kidding me? I'm the deepest brotha you know."

"Really. Then if you're so deep why are you worried about a young dude like Dilly? He doesn't have anything on you, right?"

Sam grins. "He doesn't have anything on me. As long as you know that, I'm good."

"If you're good, then I'm good."

We're good, so nothing else needs to be said.

22

Sam and I meet back up with everyone at the hotel, in Big D's suite after the concert is over. I've got my hair pulled up into a wet ponytail, and I've changed into sweat shorts and a tiny tee.

"You look refreshed," Big D says as we all pile into the suite.

"Thank you!" I say. "I feel a lot better. Relaxed."

Too bad we didn't take Dreya with us to the spa. She's on a rampage about something new. Apparently, a blogger is up in her business again. You would think she'd get tired of going from one tirade to the next, but she doesn't.

"What's wrong now?" I ask Big D.

He replies, "Some Atlanta blogger said that she was a high school dropout."

I cover my mouth with my hand. "Wow! I see why she's mad. There's a huge difference between flunking twelfth grade and dropping out of school."

Sam reads the blog post out loud. "Our secret spies tell us that Epsilon recording artist Drama was out with the rest of her tour-mates when they started celebrating her cousin Sunday's graduation. Our sources say that while Sunday was there in her cap and gown, Drama sat in a corner pouting, talking about her tutor. Wonder what Epsilon will do about the juvenile delinquent on their record label. That's a real example for the kids, right?"

"Wow," is all I can muster. That article is a hot crazy mess.

Bethany scoffs, "They didn't even mention that we celebrated my graduation too!"

"Nobody knows who you are," Dilly says. "That's why they didn't mention you."

"I just like how they said I was wearing a cap and gown. I so didn't have that on," I say.

Dreya paces back and forth across the floor. "Get that camera out of here!"

"We have a right to be here," Chad, the producer, says. "You signed a contract and there's no way we're missing this meltdown."

Big D says, "Listen, man. You've got enough footage of this. Either you leave or I have you forcefully removed."

"I will be reporting this to Epsilon Records," Chad says.

"Go ahead. I guarantee you that they don't want this portrayed on their show. I know that without a doubt."

Chad reluctantly leaves with his cameraman. Big D then forces Dreya to sit down on the big fluffy chair on the side of his bed.

"Drama, chill out. We know you didn't drop out of school. There's no need to get all twisted over a lie."

"I'm not twisted about the story. I'm twisted that somebody in our camp is a snitch. I think someone is feeding this stuff to the bloggers."

Her eyes fall on every person in the room. Me, Sam, Bethany, Truth, Big D, Shelly, Regina, and Dilly. I don't think any one of us would do anything to jeopardize the tour, but I don't think she sees it like that. But Dreya only ever sees what she wants to see.

My telephone rings. "Hey, Mystique."

"Hi, Sunday. Are you in the same room with Drama and the rest of the crew?"

"Yes."

"Excuse yourself and walk back to your own room. Then call me."

"Is everything okay?" I ask.

She replies, "Yes. It's time for a little damage control. Epsilon Records is breathing down my neck about this Internet story."

"Hey, y'all, I'll be right back," I say after pressing End on my cell phone.

"Where are you going?" Dreya asks. "Off to tell the bloggers more lies about me?"

I shake my head. "Actually, no. But if you want I can tell them lots about you. Stuff that you'll know I told, because no one else knows about it."

Dreya does not want to go there with me. I know all kinds of stuff about her that would make the Internet bloggers drool. Ooh, I know. How about the case of chlamydia she caught in the eleventh grade, from another girl's boyfriend? Yeah, that's a good one.

She soooo doesn't want to rumble with me.

Once I'm in my hotel room, I pull out my cell phone and call Mystique back. "Hey. It's me."

Mystique says, "I'm going to conference you with Atlanta Spyce."

"What? I don't want to talk to her."

"Yes, you do. If you want this tour to keep its sponsors, then you most definitely want to talk to her."

"But she's the blogger who posted the story about Dreya."

"Yes, and she's willing to retract it, if the denial comes directly from you or Drama. I didn't think your cousin would do it."

I sigh loudly and plop down on my bed. "Okay, go ahead and call her."

Mystique puts me on hold while she dials. I guess it's not enough for me not to have any scandals of my own. Now I have to clear up mess that has to do with Dreya. Wonderful.

Mystique clicks back over. "Okay, I have Spyce on the line."

"Hey, Spyce," I say cheerfully. "How are you?"

The woman laughs a throaty laugh. She sounds like my grandmama. I don't know why I thought she'd be a young person.

"I'll be better once I get this interview. Y'all are gonna get my hit count up to a million hits today."

"Glad we could help," I say in my sarcastic tone. There's something creepy about the woman. I can almost imagine her slithering around on the floor wherever she is.

"So tell me, Sunday, did your cousin, Drama, drop out of high school?"

"No, she did not. She missed a lot of school our senior year, recording her album and doing promo dates. She's only a half credit away from graduating."

"Our sources tell us that she didn't graduate because she cheated on her final English exam and someone gave her a fake cheat sheet."

I take a huge gulp. Is Bethany the one feeding dirt to the bloggers? She's the only one, besides me, who knows about Dreya's cheating.

"That's ludicrous," I say, the lie burning the roof of my mouth as it comes out. "Dreya is so passionate about education. She'd never do that. In fact, she's working with her tutor right now to make sure she gets her diploma as soon as possible."

"That's good to know. I hear you're college bound."

"Yep. I'm going to Spelman College in Atlanta."

"What about Drama? Is she attending Spelman too?"

"Um, no. I think she'll probably think of college after she's done promoting her current album and releasing her sophomore album."

"You are a great spokesperson for your cousin," Spyce says. "You should be in public relations. It's a shame we couldn't get her on the line."

"She's so broken up about the story. I don't think she would've given you a good interview," I say truthfully.

The interview Dreya would've given would've just been full of curse words and insults. Spyce better hope that Dreya doesn't see her out and about.

Mystique says, "Okay, Spyce, that should be enough to clear up anything. You good?"

"I'm good. Thank you, Mystique. I'm one of your biggest fans, you know that right?"

Mystique replies, "Thank you, girl. I sure appreciate you."

Mystique disconnects Spyce. Then she says, "You know what? Hang up and call me right back. I want to make sure the line is clear."

I do what Mystique says, and she answers on the first ring. "Okay, cool. Good interview, Sunday. That ought to help your messy cousin."

"I hope so. It was a lie anyway. She didn't drop out of school. I think she was really trying hard to graduate."

"I don't care about that," Mystique says. "Drama is living up to her name, and Epsilon is not feeling it. She needs to be careful."

"Yeah, I know."

"How did the show go in Jacksonville Beach?"

I perk up at the new topic. "It was fun. My microphone went out on me just as we were about to start. But we had some fun with it. Dilly got a chance to freestyle."

"I know. He called and told Zac," Mystique says. "He was so excited. He said the crowd was pumped."

"They liked him for sure."

"I think Zac might move the release date for his album up some. He's starting to think that Dilly might be what people want right now."

"Cool!"

"I think he has a huge crush on you, too, Sunday."

Now why would Mystique drop that on me out of nowhere? I don't need to hear that Dilly has a crush on me. It's already hard enough holding a conversation with him and those dreamy eyes.

"He does not!" I say. "He just tried to holla at Bethany the other day."

"Probably because he thought you'd tell him to bounce. It would be great for the label if y'all explored that. Y'all would be the teen-friendly version of Truth and Drama."

It sounds good and everything, and Dilly's hot enough and about to have a huge career. But slowly and surely Sam is re-staking his claim on my heart. I don't want to hurt him again.

"I don't think so, Mystique. We're friends, that's about it."

"Well, don't count it out. Have fun in Charlotte. Call me after the show and tell me how it went."

"Okay, 'bye."

Before I can even disconnect the call there is a pounding on my hotel room door. Whoever this is better have a good reason for making all this noise.

"Sunday, open up. I know you're in there with your sneaky self." This is Dreya's big mouth.

I open the door, and it's not just Dreya. Truth, Big D, and Sam are right behind her.

"Atlanta Spyce posted your interview," Sam says.

"Already?"

Sam replies, "Yeah, we were reading the comments and when I hit refresh, it was there with the title, 'Breaking News.' "

"I don't need you explaining anything for me," Dreya

says. "If Atlanta Spyce wants answers about my life then she needs to come to me and not you."

"She didn't come to me," I explain. "Mystique went to her. She's trying to save your career, dummy."

"Mystique isn't trying to save my career. She's trying to make you look like a goody-goody, so you can help her and her man keep stacking paper. She doesn't care about me."

"Okay, then, Dreya, whatever. I'm tired, and I just want to take a nap in a real bed before we have to get on the tour bus tonight."

"Yeah, whatever. You and Mystique need to remember who you're messing with."

I give them a weak hand wave and close my hotel room door. I'm deliriously tired now, after all this drama. I stumble over to my bed and fall in, fully dressed. Right before I close my eyes I think about my cousin again. She better figure out real quickly who has her back and who wants to take her spot.

23

I guess Dreya is all fussed out when we get on the tour bus. She and Truth sit huddled up in the back of the bus, and she's knocked out. Good thing for the rest of us, because we're all tired of hearing her mouth.

Dilly plops himself down in the empty seat in front of me. It surprises me a little bit when his face pops up over the back of the seat. Instinctively I check and see where Sam is on the bus. He's with Big D at the front of the bus, holding a portable keyboard across his lap. They're probably talking about beats or something.

"You rock for that shout out you gave me tonight. I could kiss you for that."

I laugh out loud. "Okay, but please don't. I don't want you to get manhandled on the bus."

"By who? Sam? The dude that played you for that skanky girl? The one who was supposed to be your prom date, but then you had to ask me at the last minute? That dude?"

"When you put it like that he sounds like some kind of dog," I reply.

"If it walks like a dog, barks like a dog . . ."

I roll my eyes. "Point made."

"Anyway, I just want you to know I appreciate what you did. You didn't have to do that for me. You could've just treated me like a stagehand."

"It's not a big deal. I'd do it for anybody."

He smiles. "I don't think you would. I think you did it because you like me."

"I do like you, Dilly. You're a nice guy."

He shakes his head. "No. You *like* me like me. And it's okay. I won't tell anyone if you don't want me to. It can be our little secret."

"I don't like you like that, Dilly."

"I'm Romeo, and you're Juliet."

I let out a little giggle, "Boy, hush. I'm going to college; you're still in high school. How would that even work?"

"I like cougars."

I throw a pillow at Dilly's face. "Boy, stop."

"What's that? Are we getting pulled over?"

Bright lights flash behind the bus, and yes, it's most definitely a police car. It doesn't feel like we're speeding, so I wonder what this is about.

The bus driver pulls over, and a police officer boards the bus. I can't hear what he's saying to the driver, but I do see the driver pulling out his license and handing it to the police officer.

The officer walks down the aisle in the center of the bus, and flashes his light in everyone's face, although the interior bus lights are already on. Big D and Sam look mad enough to spit, but Bethany, Regina, and Shelly haven't even woken up from their sleeping.

When they get to the back of the bus where Dreya and Truth are, there is a commotion. Of course, there'd be a commotion. They've awakened the slumbering diva.

"What y'all doin' with that flashlight?" Dreya asks groggily.

"Miss, I'm a police officer. You and your fella need to step out of this seat with your hands up."

Big D stands. "With their hands up? What have they done?"

The police officer spins on Big D. "Settle down. We've got an anonymous tip that there are drugs on this bus."

"Drugs! I don't use drugs, so I know you're not coming for me."

"You speak when you're spoken to."

The police officer pulls out a walkie-talkie radio. "About to complete a search on the tour bus."

Big D starts walking toward the police officer. "You are not authorized to do a search on this bus. Where is your warrant?"

The police officer waves a sheet of paper in Big D's face. "Oh, I've got a warrant."

"What?" Truth fusses.

"You're going to have a seat right here where I can watch you, while my fellow officers search every piece of luggage on this bus."

Three more police officers board the bus and remove

all of our carry-on bags. Then they get the bus driver to open the bottom storage area on the bus.

It seems like forever that this police officer is hovering over us looking crazy. Then, finally his walkie-talkie goes off in his pocket.

The voice on the radio says, "We've found something. You're gonna want to come out and look at this."

"Nobody move. I'll be right back," the officer says.

Now everyone's awake as the officer goes off the bus.

Bethany asks, "What's going on? Are they gonna let us go?"

"I don't know," Big D says. "That all depends on what they found out there."

Finally the police officer comes back on board and holds Truth's oversize backpack in the air.

The officer says, "Whose property is this?"

"Mine," Truth replies, "but I ain't got no drugs, man."

In one swift, fluid motion the police officer has his handcuffs off his belt and onto Truth's wrists.

He says, "You have the right to remain silent. Anything you say can and will be used against you in a court of law. You have the right to speak to an attorney, and to have an attorney present during any questioning. If you cannot afford a lawyer, one will be provided for you at government expense."

"You can't arrest my boyfriend!" Dreya screams.

Big D rushes down the aisle. "Wait a minute! What did you find on my tour bus?"

"Come and see for yourself."

The police officer motions for Big D to move aside while he pushes Truth off the bus. Big D steps off the bus behind the officer, and Dreya runs behind him. The rest of us are glued to the bus windows, trying to make out what they've found.

One of the officers picks up Truth's bag and shows it to the one who was on the bus. He nods his head a few times and says something to Truth. Truth doesn't seem to respond, and the next thing we know the police officer is pushing him into a squad car.

Big D is yelling something at the arresting officer, and one of the others touches him on the arm. He snatches his arm away and trudges back to the bus as the car drives off. The remaining police officers pile into their cars and drive off too, leaving all of our luggage scattered on the side of the road.

Everyone is silent when Big D gets back on the bus. He says, "They've arrested Truth for possession of marijuana with the intent to sell. They claim they found a lot of it in his bag."

Dreya bursts into tears. "We can't leave him here! What if something happens to him while they have him locked up?"

"No, we can't leave him here," Big D says as he paces up and down the aisle. "Sam, Dilly, can y'all go help the stage crew put the stuff back on the bus?"

Sam pats Big D on the back as he gets off the bus. Dilly shakes his head sadly. Everyone is feeling the brunt of this arrest.

"We can't leave him, but we can't let Epsilon Records down on this tour," Big D says. "We've got to show up at the next show in Charlotte."

"It's the weekend, baby," Shelly says. "You ain't gonna

be able to get him out of lockup for a few days at least. Monday at the earliest."

"So we should just go to Charlotte then," Big D says.

Dreya replies, "If you leave my man here, I'm not performing anyway. So you gonna be down the two stars of your show. Good luck, Sunday. You're gonna have to perform for two hours."

"Maybe we should call Mystique," I suggest. "She'll know what to do."

Big D says, "No. Let me think. I can't let Mystique know I messed this up. This is my come up on the line too, Drama. So stop just thinking about you and Truth."

"What if Dilly performs?" Regina asks. "The crowd loved him in Jacksonville."

"That might work if we had music for him," Big D says.

"Sam can whip him up some tracks or something," Bethany adds. "He's good at that on the fly."

Why are they standing here floundering when all we have to do is call Mystique? She can get her hands on music for Dilly. He's got an entire album completed. I know this is Big D's chance to show he's got what it takes, but bottom line, he didn't keep his artists in check.

"If you do stay here," I ask, "how are you gonna get around? Don't you need to think about renting a car or something? And a hotel for you and Dreya?"

"Drama's going to Charlotte with y'all. She's gonna perform," Big D says.

"I'm not going anywhere without my man. I'm ride or die for Truth. What I look like not holdin' it down for my man!"

"I know that's right, girl," Bethany says. "That's your boo."

Shelly adds, "I wouldn't leave you, Big D."

OMG. Why is Shelly chiming in on this foolishness? It's not like Truth is in jail in a third world country or even in the backwoods! He's in Columbia, South Carolina. I saw a welcome to Columbia sign right before we got pulled over.

Big D looks completely worn out as he runs a hand over his head. "All right then, stay. Sunday, get Mystique on the phone. There's no other way."

I press in her number. It's late so I don't expect her to answer right away. Finally, after five rings she answers.

"Sunday, what's wrong?"

"Hey, Mystique. How do you know something is wrong?"

"Because it's two in the morning and you're calling my cell. What's up?"

I spill the entire story, with everyone's eyes on me. Big D looks especially nervous about what Mystique might say or do.

"Tell Big D to see about him," Mystique says. "I'll meet y'all in Charlotte. Shelly can make sure y'all get there okay, right?"

"I think so."

"And Sunday," Mystique says, "tell Big D not to worry about this. There's nothing he could've done to prevent it. We'll handle it."

"Okay."

"I'm going to bed now. I'm gonna have to catch the first flight out of here. Get some rest."

I get off the phone and tell everyone what Mystique said. Big D looks relieved, but Dreya looks heated. In fact, she looks like she's about to get to blowing up in here at any second.

"It's just Queen Mystique to the rescue, huh?" Dreya says.

"What's wrong with that?" I ask, feeling extra protective of Mystique right now since she's the one bailing us out with Epsilon Records.

"I think she's the one who set my man up. That's what's wrong with it."

Big D shakes his head angrily and says, "Are you out of your mind? Why would Mystique do that?"

"All I know is the police get an anonymous tip, and next thing you know, Mystique is the clean-up crew. She thinks somebody is stupid. For real."

Somebody is stupid. And everybody on this bus is looking at her with blank stares. Even the one who I suspect *really* set Truth up. I just need a little bit more proof before I'm sure, but I think our snitch is Bethany.

24

We get to Charlotte late, of course, because we were delayed on the road. But we get in town around noon and are able to check into the hotel. Because we were so late, we ended up getting to the hotel at the same time as Mystique. She's not staying here, though. She only stays at five-star hotels, and we're in a Courtyard Marriott. Nice enough, but not top of the line.

Benji and Mystique are waiting for us in the lobby as we bring in all of our bags. When she sees me, she runs up to give me a hug.

"You okay?" Mystique asks. "You sounded really stressed on the phone last night."

"I was really stressed. Everybody was, especially Dreya."

I think about Dreya's accusation of Mystique again. There's no way in the world Mystique would put any of us through this. She doesn't even roll like that. Maybe it was the stress that made Dreya think that, because it doesn't even make sense.

Mystique waves Shelly over after she gets everyone's hotel room keys. She says, "Shelly, I just got off the phone with the concert promoter. He's pissed that neither Truth nor Drama are gonna be here. I offered to perform in their place."

"You did? That's a come up for him."

"Yeah, but he still tried to act like he wanted to sue Epsilon Records. Even though he wouldn't have much of a case against Truth, he might be able to come after Drama, since she chose to be detained in another city."

I shake my head. "That's dirty! He's getting you in place of Drama? He's guaranteed to sell more tickets if he hasn't already sold out."

"He hasn't sold out. But I told him that I'd sweeten up the pot, and Zac would come too."

Dilly overhears and leans in to kiss Mystique's cheek. "A Zillionaire concert. Wow, that's rare."

"Yeah, just pray he does it. He might be mad at me for offering it, but he'll understand once I tell him everything that happened."

Mystique pulls Shelly by the arm. "Hey, y'all, I need to speak with Shelly in private for a minute. Sunday, get settled in your room, and I'll come see about you in a few. What room are you in?"

I look down at my keycard. "Five twenty seven."

"Okay. See you in a few."

I watch Mystique and Shelly walk off arm and arm,

and wonder what they could possibly have to talk about that everyone else can't hear.

"Five twenty seven, huh," Sam says as he grabs one of my bags. "I'm in five twenty nine. Wonder if we have adjoining rooms."

"If we do, my side of it is staying locked!" I reply.

Sam laughs. "You're so cold to a brotha. I'm just tryin' to get in where I fit in."

"Sunday," Bethany says, "do you want some company tonight?"

Bethany hates that she has to stay in a hotel room with two dancers and Regina. They sleep two to a queen bed. The dancers are cousins, which leaves Bethany bunking with Regina. When Dreya is here, she always lets Bethany use her room, because it's either a suite or she's off in Truth's room anyway for the night.

"Yes, please take her in your room," Regina says. "She kicks like the devil. Last time I shared a bed with her my ribs were bruised in the morning."

I cover my mouth with my hand to hold in my giggle. "You're lying, Regina."

"I swear on everything, I'm not. It's like she thinks she and that supersonic donk she's carrying around is entitled to extra space."

"Let's go upstairs," Sam says. "I'm gonna order some pizza for lunch, and we can just chill for a minute, since y'all don't perform tonight."

"We've got interviews in the morning, though," I remind him.

"But at least you don't have to go on stage until tomorrow night."

"True that. Come on, Bethany. You can stay with me. Maybe we'll get a chance to talk about your music."

Her eyes widen and light up. "Okay, cool."

Sam looks at me with questions in his eyes. I give him a dismissive head shake. I'll explain it later. I wish I didn't have to explain it at all.

Once we get in my room, Sam makes me sit down, and he unpacks some of my stuff. I stop him when he holds up a pair of my panties. My underwear is classified, top secret information. Definitely a no-boys zone.

Sam flips through the informational book that's in most hotel rooms until he finds the number to a pizzeria. He pulls out his cell phone and dials the number.

"What do you want on your pizza?" he asks. "You too, Bethany?"

"I like pepperoni, mushrooms, black olives, green peppers, and onions," I say.

"Dang, all of that?" Sam asks with a laugh. "What about you, Bethany?"

"Ham, sausage, pineapple," she replies as she sits down on the edge of her bed.

"What y'all think Dilly wants?"

"Plain pepperoni is always safe," Bethany says.

Sam orders the pizza, and Bethany looks at me like she wants to say something. She even opens up her mouth, but then she closes it again.

"What's up?" I ask, knowing her too well to let this go.

"Nothing," she says. "I was just gonna say, I'm happy we're sharing a room. Maybe we can play Scrabble or something."

"I don't have any board games!" I said. "Do you?"

She nods. "I've got Scrabble and Monopoly. Maybe Monopoly would be good. Everybody knows how to play already."

"Yeah, I guess that will be cool."

Sam says, "I'm going down to the lobby to wait for the pizza. I'll be back upstairs with Dilly when it gets here. They said thirty to forty-five minutes."

"Why does pizza always take so long?" I ask. "My stomach is about to eat my ribs."

Bethany laughs out loud. "I've got a bag of chips in my bag. You want it?"

I don't know how I feel about Bethany's being nice. Part of me wants to think maybe we can be cool again, but the other part of me feels like this is a survival technique. Dreya's not here to have her back so she's got to be friendly to us. If Dreya was here, they'd probably be posted up somewhere ordering expensive sushi, thinking they were too good for a little greasy pizza.

"I wonder if Dreya is okay," Bethany says.

I reply, "She'll be all right. Big D is with her."

I know she's gonna be mad when I ask her this, but I'm asking anyway, because I've got to know.

"Bethany, are you the snitch? Are you the one who called the police on Truth?"

She looks completely shocked like I came out of left field with the question. But I don't know if she's surprised I would accuse her or surprised she got caught.

"No! Why would I do that to Truth?"

"I don't know, but first the fact that Dreya flunked got leaked to the Internet blogs."

Bethany drops her head. "That was me. But I didn't do this thing with Truth."

"Are you serious? You're the one who told the bloggers about that? But why?"

Bethany holds her head up with her nose aloofly pointed to the sky. "Dreya threw a shoe at me, and that day I just snapped. She's very abusive, and some days I just don't feel like taking it."

"What about the cheat sheet thing? Did you play Dreya with that, too?"

Bethany shakes her head. "Naw. I really did study for my final, because the girl I got the cheat sheet from wasn't reliable. She's given me bum sheets before. Dreya knew she was risking it. That's her bad."

Wow! Who knew that Bethany had some vengeance tucked away in her little fearful heart? She sure got her back good. Nobody would argue with that.

"But you didn't snitch on Truth."

"Nah, I'd never want him arrested. Contrary to what you think, he's actually a really nice guy. He always treated me well when we were alone."

"Did you think you were like his side piece or something?" I ask incredulously. I'ma need her to find some self-esteem.

"Some of it was because he said he'd hook me up with a deal, but part of it was because I really like Truth. He's funny and smart, and . . ."

"Ew! Ew! Ew! Enough! It's bad enough I had to see you kissing him, I don't need to hear you drooling over him too. That's too much."

"Sorry."

There's a knock on my hotel room door, and it's Sam and Dilly with the food. Thank God. If I stayed here any longer with just her I probably would've choked her out with all that crazy talk.

"Pizza, yo!" Sam says.

"Hey, Sunday, Bethany. I heard we were playing Monopoly."

I nod. "Yeah, but let me get at that pizza first."

We all stuff our faces with pizza. I can only eat three slices but try to eat more. Sam has five, and Dilly has dang near a whole pizza. Bethany only eats a couple slices.

"Y'all ready for Monopoly?" Bethany asks.

"Yeah, why not," I say through a yawn. I'm actually too whipped to play Monopoly, but I'll go along with it for the moment.

Before she even sets the board up on the bed, I'm dozing off.

"Sunday, girl, go to sleep," Sam says. "You'll be awake in the morning doing an interview, and we'll be sleeping in."

Bethany giggles, "Yeah, Sunday. You can go to sleep, and I'll keep the boys company."

This makes me sit straight up in the bed.

Bethany sucks her teeth. "Dang, Sunday, I'm just playing."

I stretch and reach both my hands over my head. I loosen up my ponytail holder and let my thick hair fall over my shoulder. I really am sleepy, but I don't think I can go to bed with a party going on next to me.

I think Sam senses this because he says, "Come on,

Dilly, let's take a rain check on the Monopoly game. I'll have to beat you at it some other time, Bethany."

"Okay," she says. "We've got to make sure that the princess gets her beauty sleep."

This is the Bethany that I've come to know over the last few months. This is hater Bethany who's become closer to Dreya and farther away from me. I knew she'd show herself in a little bit. All we had to do was keep the conversation going, and she appeared.

"She is not a princess," Sam says.

"I know, right?" Bethany responds. "I don't think we should not have fun just because Sunday needs a nappy wappy."

"She's not a princess, she's a queen. And she's running this right now. See you in the morning, Your Highness," Sam replies.

He walks over and kisses me on the forehead. Personally, I think this display was for Dilly's sake so he can know what it is, but it's still really nice. Every day I spend with Sam on this tour, he just keeps racking up the cool points.

Maybe by the end of the tour he will have scored himself a girlfriend.

25

It's been a couple of days since I talked to my mother on the phone. I didn't know if I wanted to tell her about Truth getting arrested, and I still don't know if I want to give her all of those details. But I do need to check in before she starts getting worried about me.

"Hey, Mommy," I say as soon as she picks up the phone.

"Sunday. Long time no hear from. What city are you in now?"

I can immediately tell by the tone of my mother's voice that something isn't right at home. She usually tries to keep her worries to herself, but I know her better than anyone. I'd recognize that quiver in her voice anywhere.

"We're in Charlotte. We've got a show tonight."

"I've heard Charlotte is a nice city. I'd like to visit it sometime."

"Mommy, it's not far from Atlanta. We should take a road trip and go."

"Maybe we will."

I clear my throat, "Ma, how's Aunt Charlie and Manny?"

"Manny's bad as ever. I'm telling you I had to whip his little behind twice yesterday for sassing me. I don't know where he gets it from. Neither you nor Dreya had that much mouth when y'all was his age."

"He watches videos and *The Real Housewives* all day with Aunt Charlie. That's where he got that smart mouth."

My mother laughs. "True, true. He's gonna be a nightmare for those teachers in kindgergarten."

"I know! Somebody is gonna be calling Aunt Charlie on a daily basis."

"Where's Dreya? Let me speak to her."

"Um . . . er . . . uh . . . she's not here."

My mother's tone deepens. "She's not there with you by the phone, or she's not in Charlotte?"

"She's not in Charlotte."

"What!"

I explain to my mother about Truth getting arrested and how Dreya, Truth, and Big D were going to meet us at our next stop in Columbus, Ohio.

"If Big D's in Columbia, then what adult supervision do y'all have?" my mother asks, sounding truly worried.

"Shelly's with us, and Mystique flew in this morning with her bodyguard."

"Who is that big booty girl supposed to be supervising? At least Mystique is there. She'll handle business at least."

"Mommy, why did you sound upset when I first called?" I ask.

"It's nothing for you to worry about."

"Mommy . . ."

"LaKeisha and her crew are at it again. One of them heifers keyed up my car while it was in the driveway."

This makes me furious! "Mommy, when I get my check, I'ma get you a new car."

"No, you're not. You're going to add it to your college tuition. When you get your entertainment law degree, then buy me a car."

"Deal. But you should call the police on LaKeisha and them."

"I've got it handled, baby. Don't worry about it. As long as they don't put their hands on me, or mine, it's all good. I can replace a car."

"Okay, Mommy. We have to perform in a few minutes."

"All right, tell everyone I said behave. Tell Bethany to keep her clothes on."

I laugh out loud. "I will."

Mystique is wearing an all sheer bodysuit for her performance. The suit has gold material where her nude body parts might show. From behind, it looks like she's got on a pair of shiny golden boy shorts. The whole look is too risqué for my liking, but Mystique and her six-inch heels make it look glamorous.

"What do you think?" she asks.

"You look flawless. You make me want to go back and find something shiny to put on. I feel dull standing next to you."

Mystique blinks rapidly a few times, causing her glitter mascara to sparkle. "My man is here. I've got to look hot."

Zac is on the other side of the room, talking to Dilly. It looks like an important conversation with the way Zac's arms are flailing about as he speaks.

"What are they talking about?" I ask.

"Dilly's performance. He's gonna do three songs tonight. The crowd's reaction is going to dictate whether his album stays on hold or gets released."

"Oh. Well, I hope he does well."

Mystique winks at me. "He will."

Mystique was right. Dilly didn't just do well—he was fantastic. After the show, everyone congratulates him on how the crowd was eating up his lyrics. Surprisingly, even Sam gives him props.

"You did your thang out there," Sam says. "I'd like to work on a couple of songs on your album. I've got some beats you'd like."

Dilly beams at Sam appreciatively. "Of course, I'd love to work with you. That's what's up!"

"You were soooo good," Bethany coos. "I think you might even be better than Truth."

A hush falls over the group. I guess no one wanted to admit what everyone was thinking. Dilly's set was much better than Truth's set. And with Truth having legal woes, it might be easier to do a quick swap and kick him to the door.

I just hate that the BET camera guy is here for this moment. Now it can't be taken back, and I guarantee, it'll be one of the things that shows up on the final cut.

"They've got two different styles," Sam says, trying to clean it up. "Truth is more dirty south. Heavy on the beats and hooks. Dilly reminds me of East Coast lyricists like Common, Nas, maybe even Notorious B.I.G."

Dilly's cheeks turn pink with embarrassment. "My name isn't even fit to be mentioned in the same sentence with those great emcees. Thanks, Sam. I didn't even think you liked me, much less that you were feeling my music."

"I don't really like you," Sam says with a chuckle. "But I *love* your flow. It's off the chain."

It's amazing how calm, quiet, and peaceful it is back-stage without Dreya throwing her hissy fits and Truth macking on groupies. This is the kind of tour I want to be on. One where everyone respects one another, and at the end of the day it's all about the music.

Too bad Dreya and Truth are meeting us in about twelve hours.

26

One would think that once Dreya was reunited with her man, everything would be roses. She was all lemons and vinegar when they finally rendezvoused with us at the hotel lobby in Columbus, Ohio. Big D looks exhausted, and Truth seems shell-shocked. As thuggish as he portrays himself to be, I don't think he ever set foot in a jail cell.

"How'd the show go in Charlotte?" Big D asks me.

"It went well. The crowd really loved Dilly. Zillionaire and Mystique performed too. It couldn't have been more perfect."

Dreya sucks her teeth. "How you gonna say that, Sunday? Me and Truth was supposed to be there, and you gonna say it couldn't have been more perfect?"

"I meant for the circumstances," I explain. "Stop being so dang sensitive."

"Yeah, whatever. Why was my mother blowing up my phone too? Why'd you tell them about Truth?"

I shrug. "I told my mother. I didn't know we were keeping secrets from our families."

"I'm keeping secrets from everyone until I figure out who is the snitch in this camp."

Big D shakes his head. "She's back on that again. All the way here from Charlotte, that's all she talked about. Snitches."

"Dreya, anyone could've seen what was in that bag. A hotel bellhop, one of the other hotel staff. How you gonna say for sure that there is a leak in our camp?"

"I got a feeling, that's all," Dreya says, as she plops down on a leather couch situated in the center of the lobby. "Bethany, come over here and take my shoes off. I'll walk upstairs in my bare feet."

Everyone looks at Bethany to see if she will comply. She's been pretty free the past couple of days, and she hadn't been made to be anyone else's slave in Dreya's absence.

"What's the magic word?" she asks Dreya as she kneels in front of her.

"Now, heifer. The magic word is *now*." Dreya closes her eyes, leans her head back, and thrusts her foot into Bethany's face.

I can't take this! If Bethany wants to let Dreya treat her like crap behind doors, that's her business, but if I have to see it, Dreya's gonna act like she's got some sense.

"Dreya, get your foot out of that child's face," Aunt Charlie bellows from the lobby door. "She is not your slave."

Dreya snaps up on the couch. "What are you doing here?"

"Hiring myself as the tour chaperone. Big D, you told me this Ms. Layla was going on tour with y'all. Where is she?"

Big D stammers, "S-she doesn't come on the bus or to the hotel with us. She meets us at every venue."

"What? The bus and the hotel is where y'all need the chaperones. Dreya, I'm sleeping in your hotel room."

"No, you're not!" Dreya roars. "Big D, get my uninvited mother a hotel room please."

"Aunt Charlie, you can stay in my room," I offer. Bethany frowns as I say this. Maybe she thought we'd be roomies for the rest of the tour. Not.

Dreya takes off her own shoe, snatches the hotel room key card, and marches toward the elevator, with one shoe off and one shoe on. She's in that big of a hurry to get away from her mother? Wow.

Truth's phone rings, and he eagerly answers it, like he'd been waiting for the call.

"They did?" Truth asks into the phone. "I am? . . . Will do . . . Thank you, sir."

Big D asks, "What is it?"

"The charges got dropped. Someone botched the arrest, so they can't use anything they seized against me. Without the bag, they have no case. They can't even bring it up."

Big D hugs Truth. "Man, that's all right."

A group of girls, who have been patiently hovering in the lobby, rush up on Truth like they know him.

"Aren't you Truth? The rapper?" the first girl asks.

When Truth nods, she tells her friend, "See! I told you it was him! He's just as fine in person as he is on Mediatakeout.com."

"Thank you, ladies. I appreciate y'all. Did y'all download my song from iTunes?"

They both nod frantically. " 'What Ya Gonna Do' is the hottest song I've heard in a while," the second girl says. "Will you give me an autograph?"

"Okay, you got a CD case, an autograph book, or something?" Truth asks.

The girl gives him a huge smile. "Better."

She rips open her blouse, exposing her heaving boobs spilling over her too small bra. I look away and then peek out of the corner of my eye to see if Sam is looking. He's not, but Dilly is openly gawking, like a nursing infant at lunchtime.

The first girl hands Truth a permanent marker, and he looks at it crazy. "This ain't gonna wash off for a while. You know that, right?"

"I know! Just do it!" she squeals.

So, he does. He signs the top of that girl's breast with his name. This is utter foolishness if you ask me. I've never seen anything crazier.

Apparently, neither has Dreya.

She walks back into the hotel lobby just as Truth is recapping the pen.

The girls squeal again. "It's Drama!"

Although Drama is usually very benevolent to her fans, I can tell she's only seeing red. If I were these girls, I would duck and run for cover. She's got a bottle of water in her hand, which she promptly pours over the autograph-seeker's head.

"OMG! OMG!" the girl wails. "I'm all wet!"

"If you don't get out of this lobby really quick, you're going to be wet, bloody, and sore, 'cause I'ma beat the mess outta you."

Truth tries to grab Dreya and do that little thing he always does to calm her down. But this time it is not working. She snatches her arm away while he's trying to rub on it.

"I can't believe I slept in a raggedy Super 8 Motel room for two nights waiting to bail you outta jail. This is the thanks I get for being a down for whatever chick? You pushing up on groupies right here in front of my fam?"

"It wasn't like that!" Truth says. "I wasn't pushing up on those girls. They just wanted an autograph."

Big D clears his throat. "Don't forget y'all are in a hotel lobby. You're causing a scene."

Dreya spins on her now-slippered heel and stalks over to the elevator. Truth and Big D both let out long sighs. I don't know why they're sighing now. They're the ones who created this monster!

Aunt Charlie says, "I don't know what the heck is wrong with that girl. I mean, she's always been a little spoiled, but dang! Y'all in the music business. Groupies come with the territory. Ain't that right, Bethany?"

My jaw drops! How Aunt Charlie gonna call her out like that with the cameras rolling? That was beyond foul.

"I wouldn't know, Miss Charlie." Bethany replies. "I don't really keep track of groupies all like that."

Aunt Charlie looks her up and down and says, "Oh, okay."

Everyone bursts into laughter as my aunt sashays right over and introduces herself to the television crew.

"Y'all already met me, but you might not remember, because my hair was different, and I was whoopin' somebody's behind at the time. I'm Charlie. You can call me Cha-Cha if you're fine."

Aunt Charlie backs away from the crew and holds a telephone sign up to her ear. She mouths the words *call me* to Chad the producer and confessional interviewer.

How is Aunt Charlie gonna ask why Dreya acts the way she acts? She needs to check in the mirror. Dreya is a bundle of hot mess, but that apple sure didn't fall too far from the tree.

I'm glad my mother is normal!

27

B is for Baltimore. D is for Drama. As soon as we hit the city the mess hit the fan. And I'm talking big time splatters all over the place.

We're not even off the bus yet, and it's crazy! Aunt Charlie has been chain-smoking all the way here, and so we all smell like a pack of Newports. Dreya and Truth have been bickering back and forth. Big D and Shelly had a little fight.

Just not a good day on our tour.

Dreya's on her iPhone doing her morning ritual of reading the Internet blogs. This is always an intense time for us. Because she's made herself something of a media slut, she's on Mediatakeout.com just about every day for something new.

"I do not believe this!" Dreya sounds angry, but she's laughing a little bit too. "This doesn't make any kinda sense."

"Let me see it," I say as I reach for her phone.

As I start to read the story, I'm sure my eyes are dang near bulging out of my head. It says that while we were in Charlotte that Dreya tried to hook up with Zillionaire, and that she couldn't get along with Mystique so she had a diva attack and refused to perform. It also says that Truth has beef with Zillionaire now over Dreya.

Of course this all came from one of their secret sources.

I guess somebody had to come up with a reason why Dreya and Truth were missing in action in Charlotte. But couldn't they have come up with something more believable than that? Who would believe that Zillionaire would creep on Mystique for Dreya's dusty self?

"There's not one thing true in that entire article," I comment.

Aunt Charlie says, "I'm gonna sue them. I'm tired of them going in on my baby every day."

Today Dreya is her *baby*. Yesterday she was *that heifer*. Their mother-daughter relationship is so extra sometimes! They get on my nerves.

"Miss Charlie, you're not going to sue them," Big D says. "Even though they are telling a bunch of lies, they are getting more publicity for your daughter. She's actually getting recognized when we go out now. I may have to get her and Sunday bodyguards."

This leaves a sour taste in my mouth. I don't like the idea of me walking around with my very own personal Benji. That would not be a good look, in my humble opinion, but as long as Big D thinks otherwise, there's always a chance that it might happen.

"No, thank you," I say. "I'll just take another self-defense class, to fend off my five fans."

Big D laughs. "Five fans. Girl, your singles on iTunes have already hit gold. Both of them."

"When was somebody gonna share this wondrous news with me?" I ask, somewhat indignantly.

"I just did!" Big D says.

"But it almost seems like that was accidental. You didn't plan to tell me about it. I'm not Dreya, Big D, I like to know where and when my money is stacking up."

"Why you gotta get down on me?" Dreya asks. "Isn't it bad enough the bloggers are taking shots at me? Now my own cousin is doing it too. That was not necessary, Sunday."

"No, it wasn't," I reply. "Please do forgive me."

Dreya narrows her eyes and glares at me. "You are beyond phony."

"Pretty much."

"You want to know how you can make it up to me?" Dreya asks.

"Um, no, but I think you're going to tell me anyway."

She smiles and taps her chin with her finger. "Can you call up Mystique and see if she'd set up a phone interview with me and one of those bloggers, like she did the time they lied and said I dropped out of high school?"

"I can ask her. I can't guarantee that she'll do it."

Dreya rolls her eyes as if she's annoyed. "Just call her."

Again, I call Mystique to bail Dreya out of trouble. Mystique is gonna get tired of being the clean-up woman to Dreya's mess if she isn't already.

"Hey, Sunday."

"Hey! Can you do me a huge favor?" I ask.

I hate asking Mystique to do this in front of an audience, but we're on the bus and everyone is staring.

"Depends on what you need?" I can hear the smile in Mystique's voice. She always sounds happy to hear from me, which makes it wonderfully easy for me to work with her.

"Well, Mediatakeout.com has a completely false story about Dreya in today's headlines. Something about her having a thing for Zillionaire and a diva meltdown as the reason she didn't perform in Charlotte."

"Yes, I read the story."

"I thought you didn't read them."

"I have Google Alerts set on me and Zac's names. It all depends on what the story looks like if I open it up. This one I opened."

I respond, "Then cool, you've heard about it. Dreya would like to schedule one of those interviews like we did when the bloggers made up a lie about her before."

There is a long, pregnant pause. It's so long that I think maybe Mystique has hung up the telephone.

"Hello?" I ask.

"I'm still here. You want me to set up an interview so that Dreya can debunk an Internet blogger story."

"Yeah, it doesn't have to be anything major. Just like that one we did before. Five minutes tops."

Another pause.

"Mystique, are you not thinking that's a good idea?" I ask.

"Well, I think that we've responded once to the bloggers. If we keep doing that, it'll be a never-ending cycle. They might even start making up things, just to get an interview."

"So you're not setting up an interview?" I look at Dreya and shrug. I see her face hardening into a frown.

"No. Not this time. If she wants to call them herself, she'll have to ask around for the numbers. I'm not giving them to her. Dreya is too volatile. I have no idea what she might say."

"Okay, then. I'll call you back later."

"All right, honey. Have fun in Baltimore."

I press End, and Dreya is standing over me glaring. "What did she say?"

"Not this time. She doesn't think it's a good idea."

Big D's eyebrows shoot up. "Why not?"

"She thinks the bloggers are kind of like stray dogs, and that if you keep feeding them, they'll keep coming back."

Dreya fusses, "So, let me get this straight. Mystique gets to decide how I stand up for myself? Is that right, Big D? Does she have the right?"

"She can't stop you from taking up for yourself, Dreya," I say. "She just doesn't want to be the facilitator of it."

"Don't use words I don't understand, Sunday. That's rude," Dreya says.

"Bottom line is, she's not doing it. Is that easier to understand? Is that clear?"

"What's clear is that Mystique is only interested in one person on this bus. She couldn't care less about what happens to the rest of our careers as long as Sunday is cool."

"Big D, tell her that's not true," I fuss.

Big D crosses his arms over his chest and looks at the ceiling of the bus. "I'd like to say that it's not true. But I can't be one hundred percent sure. It does seem like she's mostly concerned about you, Sunday."

"How can y'all say that when she *keeps* coming to Dreya's rescue. First with the bloggers, then she had to fly to Charlotte to be in a concert because Dreya decided to stand by her man. She does more for Dreya than she does for me."

These words sound hollow even to me. But is that so wrong that Mystique is down for me? I'm not going to apologize to Dreya or anybody else about Mystique's having my back. If they want what I got, they've got to do what I did. Find their own multi-platinum diva mentors.

28

We're in Philly now. The second to last stop on the tour. After Philadelphia, it's New York and then back home to Atlanta. The tour was supposed to be longer, but some of the venues didn't get booked, the money ran short, and all kinds of other things occurred.

To be truthful, I'm glad it's almost over. I'm tired, and I'm ready to start shopping for my college furniture. My mom and I are gonna wreck shop in Ikea! I can't wait to get some stacking shelves, beanbags, and a comfortable desk chair.

Aunt Charlie annoyed the heck out of me in Baltimore, so she's getting her own hotel room for the rest of the tour.

Sam and I get on the elevator together to go up to our rooms. He just checked in, and I'd come back downstairs for a snack. He chuckles at my handful of goodies—a bottle of Pepsi, some cheese curls, and a Three Muske-teers candy bar.

"What's funny?" I ask.

"Why don't you get some real food?"

I shrug. "I don't know where any real food is around here. What do you suggest?"

"We're in Philadelphia. How about a Philly cheese-steak?"

My stomach grumbles. "That sounds great."

"You want to catch a movie too? I heard *Eclipse* is playing at Franklin Mills Mall."

I want to laugh out loud. There is no way Sam heard that the movie was playing at the mall. Who gossips about what movies are playing? He just wants to ask me out on a date and doesn't know how. That's kind of cute, I guess. But I'ma need him to man up.

"*Eclipse?* You're a *Twilight* fan?"

"Not really, but don't all girls love those movies?"

This time I do laugh out loud. "Some girls like the *Twilight* movies. Not all of them."

"Well, forget I mentioned it. We can get a cheese-steak."

"Let me finish! I didn't get a chance to say that I am one of those girls! Let's go see it. Thank you for inviting me."

He wipes imaginary sweat off his brow. "Okay, good. I almost had a foot in mouth moment there."

"Yeah, you kinda did. But I didn't plan on letting you suffer for too long."

"Thank you for that."

"Can I ask you a question?" I ask.

"Yes."

"Is this a date we're going on? Or is this just two friends hanging out and going to the movies?"

Sam gives me a tight-lipped stare. "What do you want it to be?"

"I'm not sure."

Sam sighs. "You're never gonna be sure, are you?"

"What is that supposed to mean?" I ask.

"You know, Sunday! I've been trying to get at you for months, and you're off and on. I know you're a girl and you have the right to change your mind and all, but dang, can a brotha get something a little more solid than, 'I'm not sure?' "

A smile spreads across my face. "I will tell you what I am sure of. I'm sure that I like you. I'm sure that you smell really great right now, and I'm sure those glasses make you look like a forever nerd."

"But not sure that you want to go on a date with me?"

"I am. Let's go to the mall. Let's have a date."

Sam gives me a lopsided grin. "All right, Sunday, don't play with my emotions. I don't know if I can take it."

"I didn't say be my boyfriend! I said yes to a date."

"It's a start."

"Yes, it is."

This mall is huge. It's one of those malls you could get lost in if you get separated from your group. It's one of those malls where you see mothers with those little leashes on their bad, need-a-time-out toddlers.

And it's big enough to disappear in. Sometimes I just feel like disappearing!

Not that I'm getting recognized all that much. Dreya and Truth are starting to get a lot more of that than I am. Mostly because they're on Internet blogs regularly.

"Ooh, there's the Philly cheesesteak place." Sam exclaims.

I laugh out loud. "You sound greedy being all pumped about a sandwich."

"I feel greedy right about now. All we've been eating is Applebee's, pizza, and room service. I need some real grease lining the inside of my stomach."

"Ew."

"Right. But it's gonna taste soooo delicious sliding down into my belly." This comment wouldn't be so bad if he wasn't standing there rubbing his stomach and licking his lips.

"Tell me now. Are you going to look like the Nutty Professor some day? If so, let me out now."

"Hahahaha. You're a really funny girl!"

My phone buzzes on my hip. I take it out and read the text message that I just received.

Sunday, meet me over by the food court bathrooms.
—Carlos

I look up and around me to see if I can see where Carlos is hiding. What is he doing in Philadelphia? How does he know I'm here?

"Um . . . I've got to go to the bathroom. Order a sandwich for me."

Sam lifts an eyebrow. "You okay?"

"Yeah."

"I don't know. You read a text message, and then next thing you know, you're running off. If I didn't know any better, I'd think you were going to meet some dude."

I roll my eyes and smile. "That was from Ms. Layla. She wants me to call her later about my outfit tonight."

Wow. I've never lied to Sam before, and that just slid off my tongue. It was way too easy.

But I can't let him know that Carlos is here. Nobody is supposed to know where he is or that he's even alive. Not that I think Sam would do anything to put him in danger, but I can't play my mom out like that.

I make a zigzag path in the direction of the RESTROOM sign. I look back over my shoulder, and Sam is staring after me. He looks worried—as worried as I feel.

When I get to the women's restroom door, I glance around looking for Carlos. I don't see him, so he must be hiding somewhere. My hip buzzes again.

I'm in the women's bathroom. Handicapped stall.

This must be serious if he's hiding in a women's restroom stall. I push the heavy door open and look underneath each one for shoes. There's a lady and her two little girls at one end, and I see a pair of sneakers in the handicapped stall.

I knock on the door. "Say something, so I know it's you. If you don't, I'm running."

"It's me, Sunday."

I breathe a sigh of relief. It is Carlos.

He opens the stall door and pulls me in. "What's up with the espionage?" I ask.

"I've got to tell you something quickly, before they realize I'm gone from New York City."

His skin is pale, and his eyes bloodshot. His hair has grown longer, and it's again slicked back into a ponytail. He's lost weight too, a lot of weight.

"Dude, you ain't on that stuff, are you? You are looking really slim."

Carlos smiles. "The life I'm living now kind of does that to you. I'll be fine. How is Shawn?"

"She's cool. Your baby mama is still harassing her. LaKeisha and Charlie got into a fight right before we went on tour."

"I know. My cousins have been keeping tabs on her and the tour."

"They have?"

"They're mad how the whole marijuana thing went down. They had Dilly and Truth mixed up. They thought Truth was LaKeisha and Bryce's brother."

"They hid the stash on our bus?"

Carlos nods. "Yeah, and they called the police."

"But what do they want with Dilly?"

"That's what I came to tell you about. Now what I'm about to say is top secret. If you tell anyone what I tell you someone will get hurt."

"Okay, so what is it?"

"My cousin's gang is going to kidnap Dilly when y'all get to New York City."

"What? Oh, my God! Kidnap him?"

Carlos puts his hand over my mouth. "Shhh! Keep your voice down."

Slowly he lets his hand go from in front of my mouth. I whisper, "Why would they want to kidnap him?"

"To teach Bryce and LaKeisha a lesson. They're not going to hurt him. They're just going to snatch him and demand a ransom. Let them squirm a little bit and then set him free."

"I'm down with teaching Bryce and LaKeisha a lesson, but don't they have some kind of scared straight program or something? Dilly is my friend."

Carlos says, "Trust me when I tell you they won't hurt him. It's just that they can't let Bryce get away with what he did to me. If I hadn't survived the shooting, he and LaKeisha would already be dead."

My head is swimming. This is way too gangsta for me. I thought this craziness only happened in movies. Never, ever would I have thought I'd be in the center of a scene like this. I'm tripping the heck out.

"Why are you telling me this? Why couldn't y'all just snatch him?"

"I didn't want you to worry. He might go missing before your show in New York City. I don't want you to mess up your opportunity worrying about your friend."

"What if I tell the police? What if I tell Dilly?" I ask. These are very logical questions to me. I don't play by gang rules, and I don't see what's stopping me from walking out of this mall and doing just that.

Carlos shakes his head. "If you tell someone, and alert LaKeisha and Bryce, your mother will be in danger. You don't think they'd try to snatch Shawn or Manny if they knew Dilly was about to be taken?"

My face, I'm sure, goes white with fear. My mother is in Atlanta with those two thugs.

"And do you think they'd make a promise not to hurt my Shawn? Or Manny?" Carlos asks. "Just don't say anything. Don't get in the way when they start searching, don't answer any questions. Just know that he's gonna be all right."

"Okay. I won't say anything."

Carlos kisses my forehead. "Go check out there and make sure the restroom is empty. Then say all clear before you leave."

I do what Carlos says. The lady and her kids are gone, and there's no one else in here, so I give the all clear sign and go out of the restroom. I don't look back to see if Carlos made it out. I just put a smile on my face and try to figure out how I'm gonna fool Sam.

He waves me down as I reenter the food court. He's got our food and a table. I sit down in front of him and feel my stomach turn at the sight of the greasy, messy food. I've never been less hungry.

"You look like you've seen a ghost. Is everything okay?"

I nod. "I was just thinking about this Philadelphia audience. I heard they were a tough crowd."

Sam smiles. "Yeah, they are tough, but no tougher than Atlanta. Atlanta is one of the worst cities. Don't worry about it, you'll be cool."

"You think so?"

"Yeah, now eat up."

I swallow hard and take a bite into the sandwich. The seasoned meat flavor bursts onto my taste buds! It's delicious. My hunger is back with a vengeance.

I eat about half of the sandwich in four bites and wash it down with lemonade. I couldn't finish it if I wanted to. It's big enough for two grown men to split.

"You done?" Sam asks. "Ready for the movie?"

I'm really not in the mood for a movie anymore. Now that I'm full, I really just want to take a nap and say a prayer for my mother.

But I don't want to ruin our date. The date that Sam has been pressing me to have for months. So to the movies I go.

"You don't have to go if you don't want to," Sam says. He must have noticed something was up.

I shake my head. "I want to go! We didn't come all the way here just for a sandwich. Let's do this."

I hear my voice, and it sounds so phony. I can't even pretend that the shrilly sound coming out of my mouth is normal. It's not. I sound nervous and tense, like something bad is going to happen at any second and I'm just waiting to duck.

"Come on. Let's walk around for a minute. You don't want your stomach to poke out tomorrow night in your stage bathing suit that Ms. Layla has you wearing."

This makes me laugh. "Stage bathing suit? That's Dreya's stuff. Mine looks like regular clothes."

"Sometimes. She's put you in bodysuits and half shirts, though. You can't have a cheesesteak belly in a half shirt."

"I know, right. Let's walk around and then go to the movie theater."

How can Carlos let this go down? He's supposed to be one of the good guys. Is he so blinded by the need to get revenge on Bryce he doesn't see that this kidnapping plot is crazy? I wish he hadn't filled me in.

I push my meeting with Carlos to the back of my mind, at least for now. I can't think about Dilly being kidnapped, and not tell anyone. But since I can't tell anyone without my mother being in danger, I'm going to try to forget I even know anything about it.

It's the best I can do for now.

29

Chad, the BET guy (that's what we've been calling him), has set up a makeshift confessional in his hotel room. It's nothing more than a chair and a blue piece of material hanging from the wall. It kinda reminds me of where you have to sit to take a driver's license picture or a passport photo.

I've been sneaking out of having my confessionals, so I know he's got some irritating questions to ask me.

"The arrest, Sunday. What were your thoughts?"

Knowing what I know now about Carlos's cousins changes how I feel about that. I did think that Truth was trying to live out his rap lyrics in real life. Now I know he was set up.

"I believe that Truth was innocent. He's not the kind of guy to sell drugs."

Chad laughs. "Are you serious? The guy's a real thug."

"He's actually a pretty cool guy. Did you know he can cook?"

Chad laughs out loud. "Okay, Sunday, give me something I can work with here. What were you thinking when the police officer stepped on your bus?"

"I was thinking we were all going to jail or something crazy. I was thinking that the admissions officer at Spelman might not appreciate my having an arrest on my record. I don't know. I was thinking a whole lot of stuff."

"But Mystique and Zillionaire saved the day. They came to Charlotte?"

"Yes. They came and performed, and it was hot, and everyone liked it. The concert promoter was cool with it."

"Are you and Sam dating now?"

"Whoa. Skipping subjects. Sam and I went out on a date. Yes."

"But are you dating?"

"He's a great guy. . . ."

"Dating?"

"Huh?"

"Sunday! Dating?"

"I don't really want to discuss my personal life, you know? He's my friend. That's all y'all need to know."

Chad shakes his head. "You're the toughest one to interview. Everyone else is so open."

"Sorry for being tight-lipped. I'm a private person."

"All right. I got ya. One more question, though."

"Okay. Go ahead."

"Will you go on tour with Drama and Truth again?"

I lean my head back and have a hearty laugh. "I will never go on tour with them again!"

*   *   *

Dilly is helping me get my microphone on for tonight's concert, and he looks tired like the rest of us. I always thought touring would be a blast, and that we'd go from city to city having fun. This has been the most mentally draining time of my life.

Carlos's visit, of course, has something to do with that.

"Dilly, can you do me a favor when we get to New York City?" I ask.

"Sure. What do you need me to do, hottie?"

I chuckle. "First, you can stop calling me hottie. That is so unnecessary."

"It is. I'm sorry. What do you need me to do for you?"

"I want you to stay near Big D or Benji for the entire time."

Dilly looks at me with a strange expression. "What's wrong, Sunday?"

"Nothing. You're just too young to be all over New York by yourself. I don't want you to get lost from the group."

He laughs. "Sunday, I've been going to New York with my brother since I was a little kid. I probably know the subways better than people who live there. You don't have to worry about me getting lost."

"You said you would do me the favor. So will you?"

Dilly cocks his head to one side as if he's trying to read my mind. I'm pretty closed up right now, so even if he did have telepathic powers, he'd be up against a brick wall.

"You sure there's nothing wrong?" he asks.

"Yeah. I just had a feeling, that's all."

That's as far as I can go without spilling my guts and

telling him the whole thing. He'd have no choice but to tell his brother, and then it would be just like Carlos said. My mother could be hurt.

What's really bothering me now is that I feel like my mother is in danger whether I say something or not. Like what's gonna happen when they do snatch Dilly? Are LaKeisha and Bryce gonna try to do something to her then?

The thought of this makes me really nervous. My hands start shaking so bad that Dilly can barely get the microphone wire up my sleeve.

"Sunday?"

"It's just stage fright, Dilly. Wire me up."

"Okay."

I try to do that breathing thing that Ms. Layla showed me to calm my nerves, but it's not working. Bethany is walking toward me, and she's smiling. I'm not in the mood for having a conversation with her, but she definitely looks like she wants to chat.

Usually, her outfits at the concerts are kind of stank, but she's just got on a pair of jeans and baby tee this evening. No makeup, no crazy hairdo. Just plain old Bethany. Makes me think of back in the day.

"Hey, Sunday, you ready to go on?"

"As ready as I'm gonna be. What's up?"

"Would you think I was lame for dating a guy still in high school?"

I laugh. "Depends on the guy. Who are we talking about?"

"Dilly and I have really hit it off since we've been on

tour. He keeps asking me to go out with him, but I don't know if I should."

Bethany and I are having a conversation about boys? I can't remember the last time this happened without it ending in an argument.

"I don't know. Do you really like him or do you just want to holla at him because he's about to blow up?"

"What do you think?" she asks indignantly.

I mean, wow. How does she want me to answer this question? I know how she's done guys in the past. I remember how she got Romell coldcocked in the hallway at our school. She's like poison to boys, and Dilly is my friend. Does she really want me to go there?

When I don't respond she says, "Why won't anyone let me change? Why can't I want to be a better person? Everybody is trying to hold me to my past. It's not fair."

Well, maybe I'd believe it if the past wasn't just a couple of weeks ago. I just saw her in the closet making out with Truth! Now she wants to claim she's a better person? I've got to see more than a change in her outfit.

"Listen. Dilly is my friend. He's a nice person. He doesn't need you messing over him. So if you're not really changing for real, just leave him alone."

"Wow. Thanks for the vote of confidence."

"I'm just being real."

Ms. Layla and Dreya stop right behind us, and they're in the middle of a low-key argument. Ms. Layla apparently tried to walk away and roll the rack of clothes with her, but Dreya is in hot pursuit.

"I want to wear red!" Dreya says. "Something like what

you made Mystique. That gold sheer bodysuit. I want one of those in red."

"I'm not designing any more clothes for this tour."

Dreya whines, "But the next show is in New York City! It's got to be fire, so I've got to wear red!"

Ms. Layla gives her an exasperated glare. "Okay, I'll come up with something, but please go and get dressed! Regina still has to do your hair and makeup."

Dreya smiles as Ms. Layla walks away dragging the clothes rack behind her. Then, she turns and faces me and Bethany.

"What do you have on, Bethany? You look regular."

Bethany grins. "Yep, regular is the look I was going for."

"Not a good look, boo. We're on the Epsilon Records tour. You need to do something to your hair and put on something sexy. This is on TV."

"Nah, I'm good. I'm not in the mood for all that tonight."

Dreya frowns. "Okay, you're my assistant, and you can't be going around looking like you're about to go to the library to do a book report. Change into something hotter."

"No."

"Are you telling me no? Do you not realize that you work for me?" Dreya asks. She walks up to Bethany and sticks a finger in her chest. "Now. Change. Your. Clothes."

Bethany knocks Dreya's hand away. "Actually, I don't work for you. I work for Epsilon Records. I told Mystique about how you've been treating me, and she told me that I could be a roadie or Sunday's assistant if I want to."

"Sunday's assistant? If that's what you want, then whatever. Go for it. You think she's gonna get you a record deal, don't you? You so thirsty it don't make no sense."

"I don't care what you say, Dreya. Your words don't hurt me at all."

"It's Drama to you. Only my family calls me by my real name."

Dreya strides away, but I can tell she's hurt by Bethany's decision. And I can tell that Bethany is hurt too, by Dreya's saying that she's not family. I can't worry about how to fix their issues, though.

I've got issues of my own. And, oh. I've got a show to do.

I asked them to change the lineup of my songs for this show. I like to start with "Can U See Me." It's my favorite song off the album.

"What's up, Philly?"

The almost sellout crowd hollers back at me.

"How y'all doin' tonight? Can y'all see me from the back row?"

I get a flurry of shouts from the back row.

I chuckle. " 'Cause I really, really want y'all to see me."

And the beat drops for my song. It really makes me feel good when the crowd sings my hook with me. It's surreal that all these people can know and love a song that I wrote. It's helping me to push all the other drama I've got going on to the back of my mind.

"When I say 'Can you,' you say 'See me'! Can you?"

"SEE ME!"

"Can you?"

"SEE ME!"

I take a deep breath and smile at my fans. It's a good thing they can't really see my face from their seats. They'd wonder why I've got tears streaming down my face.

30

On our bus ride from Philadelphia to New York City, everyone is excited. Everyone except me. I can't shake this feeling of doom and gloom, this feeling that Carlos's cousins are lying and that they really might be planning to hurt Dilly. I mean, Bryce shot Carlos a bunch of times. Carlos could've died! And I'm supposed to believe that they aren't going to hurt Dilly?

If only my mother were here with me on the tour instead of Aunt Charlie. But there was no way my mother was going to use her vacation time to go on a tour.

When I inhale deeply and burn my nose hairs with cigarette smoke, I fuss at Aunt Charlie. "Can you put that out please? How are we supposed to get on stage and sing with smoke inhalation poisoning?"

"Girl, please. You been inhaling cigarette smoke since you was a baby. It ain't hurt you one bit. You been hanging around that organic, earth girl Mystique, and all of a sudden you can't tolerate a little secondhand smoke. Girl, 'bye!"

"How can you be okay with making us prone to having lung cancer? You are tripping!"

Aunt Charlie opens her window and blows the smoke out. "Is that better?"

"A little, but not much."

When Aunt Charlie sees that nobody is backing her up, she puts the cigarette all the way out in her portable ashtray. "Y'all some funny acting little divas. You and your cousin both."

Dreya fusses from her seat in the middle of the bus. "Um, don't be adding me to y'all little fight. I ain't got nothing to do with all that."

I notice how Bethany and Dilly have been hugged up and quiet in their seat near the back of the bus. They've been whispering and giggling and cuddling all the way up here. I've already said what I need to say about that, but it's still bothering me a little bit.

Finally, we make it to New York, Brooklyn actually. And we're not staying in a hotel; we're staying at Zac and Mystique's twenty thousand square foot loft. The crew is staying at a hotel, but Zac wanted to show his hospitality and have us all crash at his place.

The bus drops us off, and all of Zac's staff comes running out to take our bags inside. Most of his staff looks African or like they're from the islands. I love that because it reminds me of my mother's cousins in Barbados. We haven't been there in forever, not since I was a little girl, but I remember how they spoke and how we laughed and ate jerk chicken, peas, and rice. I'm trying to remember something pleasant right now, so I dwell on them for a minute.

Right before we go into the house, I notice a Latino man, wearing sunglasses and a jean jacket, standing a few feet from the house. He's leaning on a tree and watching us while smoking a cigarette. I feel my heart start beating really fast, because he looks just like Carlos, only a little thicker.

Big D taps me on the shoulder. "Sunday, is everything all right? You're acting strange. You're really jumpy, and you're fussing at everybody. That's not like you."

"I'm cool, Big D. I'm just ready for this tour to be over. I think I'm tired."

Big D looks up and down the street as if he's watching too. Has he heard something? Has Carlos contacted him too?

When I look back over my shoulder for the Carlos look-alike, he's gone.

"Let's go inside, Sunday. Zac's having a party later at his club, and we're all invited. Maybe you should get some rest before we go."

I nod in agreement. "Yeah, I definitely need some rest. The concert tomorrow night is gonna drain the heck out of me too."

Not just the concert. But the doom and gloom. The dark and twisty. I wish I could just fast-forward past this series of unfortunate events. First I needed a go back in time machine, and now I need a fast-forward button.

Big D and I go inside the penthouse suite. It's fantastically decorated with cream colored furniture and marble floors. The ceilings are high, and there are two skylights spilling sunshine into the wide open space.

Zac is on his cell phone and walking through his castle looking like the man in charge. He claps Big D on his back.

"Deionte! Good seeing you. You too, Sunday!" He kisses me on my cheek like we're old friends.

Then he talks into the phone. "Yeah. I want double security tonight at the club. Yeah. Big ugly lookin' dudes at the door. Yes, I want them armed. Don't send me no street dudes with guns. I want licensed security professionals . . . Yeah . . . but big and ugly."

He presses End on his phone and smiles at us. "Got to keep my artists safe, right?"

"Y'all expecting trouble tonight?" Big D asks.

"It's a holiday weekend, so yeah, we kind of are. Things can get kinda crazy here on the Fourth of July."

Mystique comes from the kitchen wearing an apron and holding a tray of cookies.

"Y'all want some chocolate chip cookies? The chef is at the club preparing for tonight, and this is all I know how to make."

Aunt Charlie jumps up and takes one of the cookies. "Thanks, sweetie. Nobody expects you to know how to cook. You're pretty enough that you really don't have to."

"Thank you, I think," Mystique says. "Have a cookie, Sunday?"

I shake my head. "No. They look good, but my stomach is upset. I've not been feeling well since we left Philadelphia."

"Do you have bubble guts from the cheesesteak?" Sam asks.

Everyone bursts into laughter. I roll my eyes and smirk at them all. "Hahahaha. No I don't have bubble guts. I think it's nerves. My stomach feels like a ball of knots."

Ms. Layla emerges from the kitchen area. "You sound like you need an aromatherapy cleanse."

"A who? A what?"

"You need to lie down flat on a hard surface with hot rocks at pressure points, while lavender lulls you to sleep."

As kooky as Ms. Layla is, that sounds pretty inviting.

"Where would I get that done? It sounds like what I need," I reply.

Aunt Charlie rolls her eyes, and snaps up another cookie. "You don't need that. You need to take your behind to the toilet and then take a nap."

Why does Aunt Charlie think the cure to every ailment is to "go to the toilet"?

"Come on, Sunday," Ms. Layla says. "We have a spa in the house, and Mystique's massage therapist is one of the best. Does anyone else want a service?"

Sam clears his throat. "Um . . . yeah, I kinda do. Is that okay?"

Ms. Layla claps her hands together. "Yes, of course! I love when men are in tune with their bodies."

She ushers Sam and I to an area of the house that rivals any day spa I've ever seen. There's some kind of instrumental music playing, and the lights are dim. There are canopies of material billowing down from the ceiling, giving the whole area a calming feel.

This is soooo what I need right now.

Ms. Layla says, "There are two mineral water showers in the back. I want you both to shower and change into the robes."

"This is tricked out!" Sam whispers to me. "I'm trying to live like this!"

Sam and I separate and go to the mineral water showers. As I step into the warm water, I try to relax. I try to tell my stomach that everything will be okay. That Dilly will be fine and that nobody will be coming after my mama.

I do feel a little bit better that Zac is getting extra security for the party at the club.

When I finish my shower, there is a petite brown girl standing outside the shower room.

"Hello, Miss Sunday. My name is Neechie. Would you like a massage?"

I nod. "I think I need one."

Neechie leads me to a room only a little bit bigger than a closet. There's a table in the middle of the floor, and the lights are dimmed.

Neechie holds up two vials of oil. "Close your eyes. When I tap your shoulder I want you to inhale deeply."

She taps my shoulder once, and I smell something that reminds me of peppermint tea and gingersnaps. The second scent smells like oranges.

"Which do you like better?"

"The first one."

She tells me to open my eyes, then taps on the table

and motions for me to lie down. Once I'm situated, she places hot rocks on my back and down the backs of my legs.

I let Neechie rub stress out of my body. Even though the stress is not gone, and the fear is not gone either, her healing hands are making it all a dull roar in the back of my mind. At least for the moment anyway.

As soon as we step in Zac's club, it'll all come rushing back.

31

Before we leave for the club, I make a call to my mother. I feel like whatever is going down, is going down tonight, and even though I can't tell her all of the details, she needs to get the heck up out of Dodge.

"Hi, Mommy," I say in my little girl voice.

"Hey, baby. You're almost done, right? The last show is tomorrow night?"

"Yes. I can't wait to come home and sleep in my own bed."

My mother laughs out loud. "You sure about that? Manny's been sneaking in your room at night."

"Aw, man! Mommy, can you wash my stuff before I get home?"

"Of course, baby. I'm just teasing you anyway. I'm looking forward to you being home."

"What are you doing tonight, Mommy? Aunt Charlie isn't there, so I know you plan on sitting in the house."

"What? How do you know I'm not going out on a date?"

"Stop playing. You already got a man."

"He's not here. So does that even count?"

I've never heard my mom talking this way about Carlos. She sounds hopeless, like she doesn't think they'll ever be together again. That makes me sad. They belong together, and he's supposed to be my stepdad. I can't stand Bryce and his goons for messing up my family.

"It does count, Mommy. Don't say that. Y'all will be back together again, real soon, I think."

"What makes you think that?"

"Just a feeling I have. That's all. Plus, I really miss having him around too, so you know . . ."

"That's all right. I miss having him around too."

"So, Mommy, do you think you and Manny could go over to Sister Helen's house tonight and hang out?"

She laughs out loud. "Sister Helen? I haven't been over there in ages. She'd probably talk me to death. I'd be over there all night."

"That's what I know. I want you to be over there all night."

There's a long silence on the phone, like my mother's trying to read between my words to see if there's anything there. Yes! I want to yell. There's something there!

"Sunday, is everything all right?" my mother asks slowly and deliberately.

"Yes, Mommy. I just want you to go somewhere other than home tonight. Please do that for me, okay?"

"Okay, Sunday. I'm going to do this, even though you

won't give me an explanation. I'm going to trust that you're asking me to do this for a reason."

"Thank you, Mommy. If there was something that I could tell you, then I would. But there's nothing that I can tell you."

"Sunday, you're scaring me."

"Don't be afraid!" I try to make my voice sound peppy. "I just want you to have some fun. You don't do that enough."

"Mmm-hmm . . . I'm praying for you, baby. You hear that. No harm or danger is going to come to you. I declare it, and I decree it in the name of Jesus."

"Thank you, Mommy."

"Sunday, I don't know what's bothering you, but I want you to believe that prayer. You hear me?"

"Yes, Mommy."

"All right. I'm going over Sister Helen's house. I think we are overdue for a visit. She'd like to see Manny too."

"Okay, I'll call you later."

" 'Bye, baby."

I press End on my phone, and I feel a little bit better. Neither my mom nor Manny are going to be in the house if anything goes down with Dilly. And no one knows where Sister Helen lives. My mother barely goes over there, so it isn't somewhere anyone would go to look for her.

Now to make sure Dilly doesn't get snatched.

32

We're treated like royalty when we step into Zac's club. I guess we are like the royal court because we are up in the club with the king and queen of the spot—Mystique and Zac.

We can barely get in good without the screaming fans asking for autographs. Zac smiles and waves, but doesn't stop. Mystique does sign a few autographs, with Benji standing guard.

With all of the people closing in on us, I can't see Dilly. This annoys me, because it was my plan to stay on him like nobody's business. I didn't want to let him out of my sight. Big D is to the right of me, and Mystique has her arm looped through my left arm. Benji's behind us, and there's a mob of fans in front of us.

Mystique screams, "Are you ready for this, Sunday?"

"Am I ready for what?"

She raises her hand above her head and waves at the crowd. "For this? Fame, fans, all of it?"

"I don't know! I'm nowhere near this status, though. I'm a long way away from this."

Mystique shakes her head. "You're closer than you think."

The BET cameras are behind us too, trying to capture this madness, I guess. I feel some comfort knowing that they're here. If something goes down, maybe they'll get it on camera.

"Let's go to the VIP area!" Mystique hollers.

My eyes dart left and right looking for Dilly. How could he have gotten away so quickly? Then I see him. He and Bethany are in the middle of the floor dancing.

I jump up and wave for him to come on with us. But he shakes his head. He motions to the dance floor with his arms and then points at Bethany's booty with his hands. She's backing up on him, and he's loving it.

I turn to Big D. "Can you go get Dilly and make him come to the VIP area with us?"

"He looks like he's having a good time. Why you try-ing to wreck my man's flow?"

I desperately try to think of something that will justify my worrying. Then I feel a hand at the small of my back. It's Sam.

"Don't worry about him," he says in my ear. "Dilly is a big boy. He won't get lost. Plus, he's got Bethany to keep him company."

I sigh, but no one can hear me, as I get pulled by Mys-tique and pushed by the crowd toward the VIP area. Maybe something I said made Big D a little worried because he and Shelly go onto the dance floor near Dilly. Now, my heartbeat slows to its regular pace.

"What's up with you, Sunday? You seem a little off. I thought my mother had my masseuse clear your aura."

"She did; let's get over to VIP. Can we see the dance floor from there?"

"We can see everything from there."

Benji leads the way for us to get into the glass-enclosed VIP area. There are plush chairs, chilled champagne bottles, and music piped in from the floor. It's like being at the club without the dusty guys breathing down your throat or getting their sweat on you.

"This is how the other side lives, huh?" I ask with a laugh.

For a while, I'm calm. There are so many people here that I can't tell if Carlos's boys are gonna be coming through or not. But I can see if anyone tries anything from my post next to the window, and I'll let security know as soon as possible.

Sam asks, "Are you enjoying yourself, Sunday?"

"I am. I just want to get tomorrow over with and get back to ATL. I'm not used to not being in control of my surroundings. And that's how I feel in New York City. I don't even know my way around here."

Zac is in the corner chilling with his friends when his cell phone rings. He steps away from them to answer it. Mystique watches him as he moves, and her face scrunches into a frown. Something isn't right about the fast way Zac starts walking toward the door to the VIP area, like he's in a hurry to get somewhere.

Zac peers out at the dance floor and frowns before

opening the door to the VIP area and leaving with Benji at his back.

I look down at the dance floor too, trying to see what Zac was seeing. And then I see him. The guy that was standing outside of Zac's penthouse when we first got to New York City. He's standing right on the dance floor, and he's moving toward Dilly.

I'm scared out of my mind, even though I can tell that Zac has already called in his security forces. Big men are moving from places all over the dance floor. The man can't see them, but from where I'm standing I can see that they have him surrounded. Dilly and Bethany are still dancing, oblivious to everything going on around them.

Benji gets to the guy first. He puts him in a chokehold and pulls him down to the floor. Once this happens it starts a chain reaction. Men come out of the woodwork to help their friend, and Benji is fighting two or three at a time.

Then, Benji gets some help from the rest of the security team. The dance floor clears as blows get thrown. I think I see a gun, but it doesn't go off, because one of the security staff intervenes and snatches the man to the floor.

I can't see Dilly, Bethany, Truth, or Dreya anymore! They must've run when the crowd headed toward the doors. But not being able to see them is driving me crazy. I start toward the VIP room door.

"Where are you going, Sunday? You can't go out there!" Sam shouts.

"I can't stay in here either. I've got to go and help."

Sam grabs both my arms and physically holds me in

place. I squirm in his hands, trying to shake myself loose
of his grip. But he won't budge. He's holding me too
tightly.

Finally, they all crash through the VIP doors. One of
the security guards has escorted all four of them and
Shelly too.

"Where's Big D?" I ask.

"He's down there fighting still. He jumped all up in it
when somebody tried to grab me," Dilly explained.

I rush over to Dilly and throw my arms around his
neck. I kiss his face over and over again. I don't care if
Sam is mad or if Bethany is jealous! I was so scared somebody was going to hurt him that it was driving me nuts.

"Dang, all I gotta do is get into a fight? Why didn't you
tell me that before? We could've done this a long time
ago."

Because everyone is looking at me like I'm an utter lu-
natic, I explain. "Carlos told me someone was going to
snatch Dilly tonight. And, he said I couldn't tell anyone
because then Bryce and LaKeisha would do something to
my mom."

Dilly snatches away from me. "What kind of people
do you think we are?" he asks.

"Your brother shot Carlos!" I yell. "That's the kind of
person your brother is! Someone who shoots people."

"I keep telling you that you don't know the whole
story but you insist on making my brother the bad guy.
I'm telling you, he might not be a saint, but he's not the
villain of this story. Believe that!"

Dilly walks to the other side of the VIP area, crosses

his arms, and stares down at the dance floor. Sam grabs me and holds me in his arms, like he never wants to stop hugging me. Some guys out on the dance floor are knocked out, and others are nursing bruises when the police officers appear on the scene.

Big D rejoins us in the VIP section. "Is everybody all right? We all here? We all accounted for?" Everyone nods. "Good. Shelly, can you get me some ice for my hand? I think I broke a finger on someone's face."

Shelly grins. "That's my boo. You put in some work baby."

I guess Dilly's not done with his tirade because he comes back over to me and Sam.

"Sunday, how can you say you're my friend and you knew that gang was about to kidnap me and you didn't say anything?" He sounds hurt, like he wants to cry. "How could you not warn me?"

"I'm supposed to pick you over my mother? That doesn't even make sense!"

"Think about it, Sunday. If you had told me, why do you think I'd tell my brother that Carlos had anything to do with it? You didn't trust me, and you almost got me hurt."

"They weren't going to hurt you."

Dilly roars furiously, "Are you kidding me? They are the Los Diablos! They would've hurt me without a thought, especially since no one knows what went down in the club that night with Carlos. They could've taken me, and it would've been your fault."

He's right. It would've been my fault for not saying

anything. But Carlos in a gang? Los Diablos? I knew his cousins were bad, but I didn't know it was like this. I want to believe that Carlos is just caught up in his revenge thing, but now I don't know for sure. Was there more to the nightclub story? Did Los Diablos have something to do with that, too?

"I-I didn't know."

"No, you didn't, but would that have been enough if I had gotten hurt?"

Sam puts a hand up. "That's enough. Everyone is scared here. She was scared for her mother, and you've got people going after you. It's not a reason for you to get all up in her face like that."

"Man, who you think you talking to? You ain't my daddy, and you don't even know me all like that. You need to fall back. I'm through with all of y'all."

"Dilly, I didn't know about it! You done with me too?" Bethany asks.

He looks her up and down and frowns. "I gotta get out of here."

Bethany starts to go after him, but Mystique, who's been silent up until now, holds her arm. "Let him go. He won't get far. Zac's men won't let him out the club." She pauses. "Sunday, you've got to trust us," Mystique says. "You could've come to me and Zac with what you knew. He's got plenty of resources for that. He could've made sure that no one got hurt."

"I know that now. But will Dilly ever forgive me?"

"We've just got to wait and see, I guess. He's pretty mad."

How do I always do this? I have absolutely no luck with friends and boys! I've got to find a way to make this up to Dilly. I just have to.

Sam hugs me again. "We'll make it better, Sunday. I'll help you do it."

I hold him tight, hoping and praying that he knows what he's talking about.

33

"They cancelled the concert," I say to Chad in my last BET confessional.

"Why did they do that?"

"A fight broke out with a New York gang the night before at the club, and the concert promoter didn't feel safe with us performing. He didn't want to take the risk of anyone getting hurt."

Chad asks, "Are you upset about it?"

"Sort of. I mean, they caught the guys that were there to do the dirt, and I really needed to perform."

"So you're back in Atlanta. What's next for Sunday Tolliver?"

"What's next for me? Well, I'm gonna chill for the rest of this summer. No more promotional tours. I'm just doing music and getting ready for college."

"Boys?"

"There you go."

Chad laughs. "I'm serious. Will you and Sam be getting closer over the rest of the summer?"

"Maybe. I don't know."

"You never give me a straight answer, do you?"

"You never ask the right questions."

I'm sitting at Pascal's with Mystique, Big D, and some guy in a suit. I take it they're going to introduce us in a minute or two, but right now everyone is just settling into the table.

"Sunday, I want you to meet Jacob Metz, my film and television agent."

I shake his hand when he offers it. "Nice to meet you."

"Sunday, he wants to talk to you about an opportunity," Big D says. "And I think you need to hear him out, because this is big."

Jacob says, "I've seen some of the footage of you from the BET reality show taping."

"Oh, my God. Is it crazy?"

Jacob laughs. "For the most part, yes! But you're not crazy in it, and that's what I'm here to talk to you about."

"Okay . . ."

"The heads over at BET are interested in giving you your own show."

My eyes widen. "My own show? Why me?"

"They like the positive image that you portray, and they want to show the music industry in a more positive light."

"What would I do on my own show?"

Mystique answers. "The cameras would tape you and

Sam in the studio and follow you around for the first couple weeks at Spelman."

There goes my idea of staying low-key on campus. I don't want to be a celebrity on campus. I just want to be a freshman.

"I don't know if I'm all that interesting."

"We'll make it interesting," Jacob says. "We'll send you to an exotic location or two for the weekend to shoot a video. Kids eat that stuff up, and you're going to college, and BET is all about that right now."

I look at Mystique and Big D. "Do you think I should do it?"

"I think you should," Big D says.

It sounds like an amazing opportunity. But what's going to happen when Dreya and Aunt Charlie find out? Are they going to hate me? Are they going to steal my joy? I don't know if I want to do this, and not have Dreya be a part in some way.

"What about my cousin?" I ask.

Jacob shakes his head. "Absolutely not. She is the opposite of what they want to show right now. A lot of what she did on y'all's reality show is going to be shown in a bad light. She's not going to be the star of that show either. You are."

I feel like I'm trapped here.

"I need to talk to my mother."

"Jacob's already talked to Ms. Tolliver, and she's all for it. She says that the money you make from the show can pay for the rest of your tuition, and she's all for that."

So, I guess it's decided then. I look at the smiles on

Mystique and Big D's faces, and they look so proud. Like parents of a baby graduating from kindergarten. It's nothing but love.

But what if I can't cut it without a supporting cast around me? What if they make me the center of attention and I bomb? I'm just about my music, and my life. There's not much reality show stuff in that right?

"What if I can't do it by myself?" I ask Mystique. "What if I'm boring?"

Mystique laughs out loud. "Sunday, you're anything but boring. Do you know how much I admire you? How much I think you are awesome? I wish I'd been like you when I was that age. You're going to be such a positive role model."

Jacob adds, "The world will be yours for the taking, Sunday. All you have to do is reach out and grab it."

I smile at them all and feel at ease now that they've gassed me up. I don't think I need Dreya, Truth, Bethany, or anybody else to help me be a star. It's time for me to step up to the plate and get my game face on.

Time for me to do it all on my own.

ALL THE WRONG MOVES

Nikki Carter

ABOUT THIS GUIDE

The following questions are intended to
enhance your group's reading of
ALL THE WRONG MOVES.

Discussion Questions

1. At the beginning of the story Sam drops a whammy on Sunday when she finds out he's going to prom with another girl. Was he dead wrong for that? Or did Sunday deserve it because she caused a fight between Sam and Truth?

2. What do you think of Dilly? Is he a possible crush for Sunday in the future or will the drama between their families keep that from ever happening?

3. Dilly tells Sunday that his brother, Bryce, is not the villain of the story. Do you think there was more to Carlos's shooting than what Sunday knows?

4. Would you be embarrassed to have Aunt Charlie for a mother? Why or why not?

5. Bethany gets really grimy in this story. Do you think Dreya will ever find out about her creeping with Truth?

6. Speaking of Bethany, do you believe that she turned over a new leaf by the end of the book? Will she and Sunday ever be good friends again?

7. What do you think is going to happen when everyone sees the reality show? Will it be drama on top of drama?

8. What's next for Sam and Sunday? They seem to be closer by the end of the book, but not boyfriend-girlfriend status yet. Will they ever get there? Or is Sunday's career going to take center stage?

Don't miss the next book in Nikki Carter's
Fab Life series

Doing My Own Thing

Available in July 2011,
wherever books are sold!

1

Have you ever been super nervous about something for absolutely no reason at all?

Today is the day when we get to see the first three episodes of our BET reality show, "Backstage: The Epsilon Records Summer Tour." I shouldn't be nervous, because I went out of my way to make sure I didn't do anything that could be misconstrued as ghetto or lame. I didn't talk badly about anybody in my confessionals, I never once used profanity, and I was only digging one boy the whole time (Sam).

So, I shouldn't be nervous.

But for some crazy reason I am. I have the butterflies-flitting-in-the-pit-of-my-stomach feeling that something ridiculous is about to pop off.

Maybe it's because I haven't really talked to anyone except Sam since the taping was completed. We ended on a bad note. The final show in New York City got cancelled because of a botched kidnapping attempt that ended up in a nightclub brawl. It was all bad.

I keep playing the whole thing over and over again in my head, because I knew about the kidnapping ahead of time, but didn't tell anyone. In hindsight, I should've tried to do something, but I was afraid that something bad might happen to my mom and little cousin. That's all I was thinking about. It didn't even occur to me that telling Big D, Mystique, or Dilly about what was going down could've led to a different result.

And now, I'm paying the price for that. Dilly's still not speaking to me, and the tour has been over for three weeks. Big D is a little salty with me too, and that really hurts, because he's always in my corner. Mystique is a little disappointed, but she told me that she would've done what I did, so that made me feel a little better.

My phone buzzes on my hip. "Hey, Sam."

"You want me to pick you up to go to the studio? Or are you driving, since you finally decided to stop being a tightwad and got yourself a car?"

I laugh out loud. Yes, I am a tightwad with the money I've earned so far on the songwriting end of things. But when I got my six thousand dollar check at the end of the tour, I went to a used car lot and got a car. It's a tricked out gold Toyota Camry that was probably seized from a drug dealer or something. Anyhoo, I'm on wheels.

"Why don't I pick you up for a change?" I ask. "I do want to drive, but I don't want to show up alone. I'm afraid I might get jumped."

"Dilly still isn't talking, huh?"

"No, and neither are Dreya and Truth, although I don't know why they're mad."

"Does Drama *need* a reason?"

I chuckle. "No, not really, but I think if someone would call her by her real name every now and then she might remember that Drama is a stage name, and that she doesn't have to live up to it."

"She will forever be Ms. Drama to me," Sam states.

"Well, whatever. She's Dreya to me. I'll pick you up in an hour. Cool?"

"Yep."

My mother calls me from the living room. "Sunday! Come here, now!"

"Sam, let me call you back. My mom is tripping on something."

Her voice sounds crazy, like she's about to try to ground me for something. But we've officially halted all punishment activities since I turned eighteen and graduated from high school. Like how's she gonna ground me when I'm helping pay bills up in here? Real talk.

But still she sounds like she's in trip out mode. I am sooo not in the mood.

"Sunday, sit down," my mom says when I come into the living room.

"What's up?"

"Look at what just came in the mail."

She hands me an envelope that's addressed to me and my mom, but doesn't have a return address. I open up the envelope, and inside is a cashier's check.

For twenty-five thousand dollars.

It's the exact amount of money that my mother's boy-friend Carlos borrowed from my college fund to buy into Club Pyramids. It's the exact amount that was stolen from him when the deal went sour and he ended up getting shot.

"Do you think this has anything to do with Carlos's cousins trying to kidnap Dilly?" she asks.

"How can we say for sure? We don't even know who sent it."

My mother replies, "It had to be Carlos. Somehow he got his hands on the money, and he's trying to make it up to you."

"But why wouldn't he let you know it was coming? I mean, he knows how to get in contact with us."

My mother sits down next to me and takes the check back. She flips it over a few times as if she's looking for clues to its origin. She sighs and shakes her head.

"Maybe it was the record company. Maybe they want all of the ghettoness surrounding you to stop, especially since they want to do a reality show with just you."

Apparently, BET liked what they saw of me from the reality show footage, and they want to give me my own show. That's all good, and I know they don't want any more brawls taking place during my new gig. But how would the head honchos at BET know about the twenty-five thousand dollars? There is no way Mystique or Big D would tell them what *really* went down at the club in New York.

"I don't think it was Epsilon Records, Mommy. They aren't really in the loop with all the drama."

"Maybe it was Big D or Mystique?"

I bite my lip and think about this for a moment. Big D is out. He's known all along about the money, and if he wanted to give it to me, he could've done it at any time. Mystique is a possibility. She's the type that would do something under the radar and not sign her name to it.

"I don't know," I finally reply. "Maybe. I'll ask them both."

My mother shakes her head. "No. Don't ask. Whoever sent this doesn't want it to be known, or else they would've signed their name. We just have to look at it for exactly what it is."

"And what's that?" I ask, completely confused at her reasoning.

"That's simple. It's a gift from God."

Hmmm . . . a gift from God? While I'm as Christian as the next person, I doubt that He's just sending random checks in the mail. If He was doing that, why wouldn't He send them to someone who really needs it? I mean, for real, I've got hundreds of thousands of dollars on the way. Isn't there some poor, single mom out there who could use the check more? I'm just saying.

But there's no way I'm gonna argue with my mother when it has to do with a blessing. She'll make me attend daily revivals, Bible study, vacation Bible school, and everything else if she even thinks I sound like I don't have faith.

So, it's up to me to figure out the identity of the mystery check writer. Something new to put on my already overflowing plate!

"Well, I guess we just need to thank the Lord," I reply.

"You sound like you're being sarcastic, Sunday."

"I'm not! If it's from God, then I think I should thank Him."

"All right. Keep it up, and your new reality show will follow you around at vacation Bible school."

This would be funny only if she didn't really mean it. Even though I'm eighteen, I'm still afraid of her. I have to hurry up and figure out the mystery check donor, before my mom makes her move.

Can somebody say a prayer for me?

Don't miss Nikki Carter's

Not a Good Look

On sale now from Dafina Books!

1

I cannot believe that it's the middle of the night and I'm thirsty. I'm parched, really—my throat feels like it's growing an afro weave.

I glance to the left of me in the dark. I can make out my cousin Dreya's shape in the twin bed on the other side of *my* room. No one can tell it's my room, since I always have to share with Dreya and her little brother, Manny.

They get on my last nerve. Honestly.

Dreya is the reason for my cotton mouth. She finds it necessary to get out of the bed every night and turn the heat up to eighty-five degrees, like she and her mama are paying any bills up in here. Nobody with human blood running through their veins needs to sleep with the heat turned up that high.

And, of course, the vent is right up over my bed. Because of this, I've been swallowing heat for the past few hours.

I throw my feet over the bed and try to escape quietly before . . .

"Sunday! I want some water."

Manny wakes up. Dang!

"Boy, you can't have no water. You're just gonna pee in the bed."

He starts whining. "But I'm thirsty."

"Boy! Go to sleep."

He squints at me and frowns. "What's wrong with yo' throat? You sound like a man!"

"I'm thirsty and my throat is dry!"

"Mine too, so hook a brotha up and get me something to drink."

"Manny, I'm gonna hurt you!"

"I'm gonna tell my mama you cussed at me."

"I did not cuss at you."

"So."

I narrow my eyes at this little evil genius. He stays trying to blackmail somebody. The other day, he got half a candy bar out of Dreya by threatening to tell that she was kissing a dude other than her boyfriend. The fact that she never actually kissed anyone meant absolutely nothing to Manny. A candy bar is a candy bar to that little hobgoblin.

"Come on then," I say, still fussing. "You better not try to get in my bed either."

"I don't even want to sleep in yo' dusty bed! I'm sleeping with my sister!"

Beautiful! The thought of this makes me smile. Dreya's gonna be heated when she wakes up to sheets soaked with Manny's pee! That almost makes up for my interrupted sleep. Ha!

Manny and I creep quietly into the kitchen, which is hard to do because we have to pass through the living room to get there. We tiptoe around feet, legs, and blankets that are spread where they shouldn't be. It's something like a hood slumber party obstacle course.

In most people's homes (I would think—since I really don't go to other people's houses at night) the living room is a pretty quiet place. Living goes on during the day, so that's when it should be busy. At night, normal people go to their bedrooms and go to sleep, and their living room is quiet.

It's a whole other story in the Tolliver household. Our tiny living room is occupied twenty-four seven. My auntie, Charlie, is sleeping on one couch and my mother's boyfriend, Carlos, is asleep on the love seat, wrapped in Manny's *Transformers* comforter.

"Gimme my blanket!" Manny hisses and tries to snatch his comforter from Carlos.

I pull Manny into the kitchen, not wanting him to wake anyone. "Stop it, Manny! You don't have a bed anyway, so it doesn't matter."

"I did at my other house."

"I wish you'd go back to your other house," I mumble under my breath.

Aunt Charlie, Dreya, and Manny moved here a year ago when they got evicted from their duplex. My aunt doesn't keep a job for longer than three weeks, and they never have enough money for rent, so they live with us off and on. It really sucks lemons.

As much as it irritates my mother that Aunt Charlie won't get and stay on her feet, she won't ever let her and her kids be homeless or on the street. That is not how Tollivers roll. We always stick together, no matter what. Even if we get on one another's last nerve.

"Sunday, I'm thirsty. Hurry up," Manny says.

I know he's not trying to have an attitude. Let him keep it up and he'll be swallowing spit.

Just for that, I take my time getting Manny's sippy cup out of the dish rack on the counter and filling it with water from the faucet. I try to hand it to him, but he shakes his head.

"I thought you wanted some water."

He shakes his head again. "Put some ice in it."

"We ain't got no ice."

"Yes, we do. My mama filled up the trays. I saw her."

I open the freezer, crack two ice cubes out of the plastic tray, and drop them into Manny's cup.

While he's drinking, I search in the refrigerator for my orange, pineapple, and banana juice. The fruity goodness that will slide down my throat in a burst of yummy flavor will be the cure for my dry, parched mouth.

I know I sound like a commercial. It was completely intentional. Plus my juice is the bidness, ya dig?

For some reason, I can't seem to find it in our refrigerator. This can only mean one thing. My beloved juice has been stolen and consumed by someone else in this house.

"Manny, who drank my juice?"

He shrugs. "How you expect me to know? I'm only four."

"Because you always asking your mama for my stuff!"

"What color was your juice?"

"What *color* was it? It was yellow!" I feel the anger rising from the pit of my stomach to my dry and crackly throat.

"Oh, that must be the juice I had tonight with my fried bologna sandwich."

AARRRGGGHHHH!!! If my throat didn't feel as dry as the Sahara Desert, I would scream that out loud, but right about now, I can only offer a raspy hiss.

I leave Manny standing there in the kitchen, with his ice water, as I storm back through the living room and down the hall. I can't stand all these people up in me and my mama's spot. I don't have anything to myself, not my own room, my own clothes. Not even a carton of juice. I wish they would all disappear!

Then I hear whimpering coming from the kitchen.

I roll my eyes and go back to get Manny. "How you gon' have all that mouth and be scared of the dark?"

"I'm not scared of the dark. I'm scared of roaches."

"We don't have roaches, Manny."

"We did at the other house."

I sigh and scoop him up into my arms. "Just come on."

I tuck Manny into the bed with Dreya and get back in my bed. I close my eyes and try to go back to sleep.

Which is impossible.

Because. I'm. Still. Thirsty!

HAVEN'T HAD ENOUGH? CHECK OUT THESE
GREAT SERIES FROM DAFINA BOOKS!

DRAMA HIGH

by L. Divine

Follow the adventures of a young sistah who's learning that
life in the hood is nothing compared to life in high school.

...ZE
...3109-1

...N'
...3115-6

...RE
...1933-4

...yal,

...T'S UP!
...2582-2

high

temptations of teen life.